blue
rider
press

shadowbahn

Other Books by Steve Erickson

Days Between Stations

Rubicon Beach

Tours of the Black Clock

Leap Year

Arc d'X

Amnesiascope

American Nomad

The Sea Came in at Midnight

Our Ecstatic Days

Zeroville

These Dreams of You

shadowbahn

steve erickson

blue rider press | new york

blue
rider
press

An imprint of Penguin Random House LLC
375 Hudson Street
New York, New York 10014

Blue Rider Press is a registered trademark
and its colophon is a trademark of Penguin Random House LLC

The author gratefully acknowledges permission to reprint lyrics from
"Trouble Down South" by the Mekons, courtesy of Low Noise America Music.

Library of Congress Cataloging-in-Publication Data

Names: Erickson, Steve, author.
Title: Shadowbahn / Steve Erickson.
Description: New York : Blue Rider Press, 2017.
Identifiers: LCCN 2016036521 | ISBN 9780735212015 (hardback)
Subjects:
BISAC: FICTION / Literary. | FICTION / Alternative History.
Classification: LCC PS3555.R47 S48 2017 | DDC 813/.54—dc23
LC record available at https://lccn.loc.gov/2016036521
p.   cm.

Printed in the United States of America
1   3   5   7   9   10   8   6   4   2

Book design by Gretchen Achilles

In those days it was either live with music or die with noise, and we chose rather desperately to live.

RALPH ELLISON

America, the plum blossoms are falling . . .
I refuse to give up my obsession.

ALLEN GINSBERG

one

shenandoah

Things don't just disappear into thin—

. . . but she hangs up on him before he finishes. "What the . . . ?" he says, staring at his cell phone in dismay and trying to remember if she ever hung up on him before. As he finishes filling the tank of his truck and replaces the pump's nozzle, Aaron ponders how this became the kind of argument where his wife hangs up on him. He hauls himself back up into the driver's seat thinking maybe this is really the kind of argument that's about something other than what it's about.

Starting the ignition, turning down the oldies station on the radio, he sits a minute irritably checking the rearview mirror. Another truck waits for him to pull away from the pump. Aaron remembers that he meant to get a donut and Red Bull from the gas station's convenience market, some concentrated discharge of sugar and caffeine to take him the rest of the way to Rapid City.

He looks at his cell to see if she's texted. "Fuck if *I'm* apologizing!" he says out loud to nobody and nothing; without his donut and Red Bull, he glides back out onto Interstate 90 in his red truck with its gold racing stripes and the bumper sticker that reads SAVE AMERICA FROM ITSELF. When he first put on the sticker, he thought he knew what it meant. The more he's thought about it since, the less sure he is.

Aaron considers the one time he fell asleep at the wheel. It couldn't have been longer than a couple of seconds, but enough to start veering off the road until another truck's horn blared him into consciousness. His heart didn't stop pounding till he finished the route: If you want to wake yourself up good for the rest of a drive, try falling asleep at the wheel for a moment. On the radio a man and woman sing to each other, not with each other, having their own argument maybe. *She hung up on* me, he's thinking, "I'm not apologizing, fuck that." But he's had fights with Cilla Ann before and knows, as his indignation subsides, that if she hasn't texted by the other side of the bridge at Chamberlain crossing the Missouri River, he'll wind up calling.

Is something else wrong? he wonders. *Is there something else going on with her?* Can this fight actually be about something as trivial as his wallet gone missing, vanished from his jacket? even if now he's a driver without an identity. The man and woman singing to each other on the radio aren't exactly arguing. It's kind of a cowboy song but not exactly, half a century old, trippy with spy-movie horn riffs—although Aaron, not caring about music, doesn't break it down like that. Instead he catches out of the corner of his ear the story that the cowboy sings in the deepest voice anyone's heard . . .

. . . of the woman seducing him with wine made of strawberries, cherries, and an angel's kiss in spring, so she can steal his silver spurs while he sleeps. *If I'm being honest,* Aaron admits to himself ruefully about the conversation with Cilla Ann, *I know it's not true that things don't just disappear into thin air. If I'm honest and I've learned anything in this life, it's that things disappear into thin air all the time.*

The woman singing on the radio reminds Aaron that these are the last days of summer, nine days before the fall.

The music that he pays little mind is only something in the background to keep him company and awake. "A song finishes," he says out loud, "ask me what I just heard, I have no idea." Sometimes instead he'll listen to the talk radio until it becomes too nuts, or the CB radio that's broken at the moment, Aaron having tried futilely back in Mitchell to get it fixed. In his early forties, he drives Interstate 90 at least three times a week counting both to and from, sometimes four or five if he can hustle up the commerce. Sometimes when the traffic of other trucks is at a maximum, or just because he feels like it, he cuts down to Highway 44 running through the plains beyond Buffalo Gap.

From the cabin of his truck, he aims himself at anything westward that he can see a hundred miles away, at the swathe of blue crushing a horizon invaded by the slightest vapor of white—not so much clouds, since there hasn't been a cloud in the sky, let alone rain, in forever. Highway 44 is draped with the flags of Disunion that grow in number the farther west Aaron gets. Later he'll wonder how it is that on this morning of the argument about the wallet disappearing into thin air, he could have missed there on the flat plain before him the two skyscrapers each a quarter mile high: the breath of Aaron's country, exhaled from the nostrils of Aaron's century.

Soon, the change in the landscape announces itself as always. Dashed lava and the blasted detritus of dying asteroids, slashes of geologic red and gold rendering his truck a chameleon. *A song finishes, I have no idea what I just heard*, but he still remembers what was playing on the radio the time he fell asleep behind the wheel, a mash-up of spirituals and national folk tunes sung by the most famous singer who ever lived: *old times there are not forgotten, look away* and *His truth is marching on* and a third, *all my trials will soon be over.*

In the two seconds when Aaron fell asleep that time, he had a dream that lasted hours, in which the song appeared as a black tunnel on the highway before him. Of course he has no idea now where the tunnel led, or whether it led anywhere or had any ending, because he woke with a great start to that warning of the other truck's horn and the open highway, no tunnel in sight.

By midafternoon—the tail end of the five-hour drive to Rapid City from Sioux Falls—Aaron has neither called his wife nor heard from her. He's buzzy and bleary at the same time, in the crossfire of fatigue and two Starbucks espressos self-administered in Chamberlain. But when he slams on the brakes of the truck, without bothering to check in the rearview mirror whether anyone is behind him, he knows he's not in the tunnel of any song. He's not dreaming the thing that suddenly has appeared before him and can no longer be missed as he rounds a corner and emerges from a pass into the Dakota Badlands, with its rocks shaped like interstellar mushrooms and ridges like the spine of a mutated iguana.

He doesn't bother pulling his truck over to the side of the highway. Stopping in the middle, he gawks for a full minute, opening and closing his eyes and then opening them again. His truck abandoned mid-highway, Aaron strides to the roadside as though the few extra feet will somehow make what he sees comprehensible; a moment later, he returns to the truck's cabin. Unsure what he would say on it anyway, he remembers the CB is dead. He pulls his cell phone from his pocket. "Hey," he says when she answers.

"Hey," he hears her say back, hesitant and quiet.

"Uh . . ."

"Look, I'm sorry. . . ." A pause, and when he doesn't reciprocate she says, "Okay then," annoyed; then another pause. "Aaron?" When he still doesn't answer, she's both irritated and worried by his silence. "Must be close to Rapid City by now."

"Listen."

"I really am sorry"—testy but maybe slightly freaked out? Sometimes he wonders if she wonders if he's going to leave her.

Listen, because he hears the music, or something like it.

The afternoon sun slides down the sky like a window shade. Aaron studies the little icons on his cell phone. "How do you take a picture with this thing?" he asks. "These things take pictures, don't they?"

"You sound like your mother," she sighs, baffled. "Tap the little symbol of the camera. Did you open the icon? So point it at whatever and press the b—"

"How do I send it to you?"

"Little arrow at the bottom . . . send it to me later. . . ."

He says, more emphatically than he's ever said anything to her, "*Now*. You have to see this and tell me—"

"Tell you . . . ?"

"—that I haven't lost my mind," but he knows he hasn't lost his mind, he's not in any dream. He's not in any tunnel; now another truck approaching in the distance from the other direction—this one's front bumper festooned with the flag of Disunion—stops in the middle of the highway too, like Aaron's. Like Aaron, the other driver gets out of the other truck to walk to the roadside, rubbing his eyes as if in a cartoon. Yet another vehicle nears, and as Aaron turns to gaze over his shoulder, up and down the highway other cars have begun to stop, passengers emerging, everyone's stupefaction surfacing in thought balloons. The sound that's like music, that Aaron thought he was hearing, he hears again: *Ask me what I just heard, I have no idea*, but not this time. "Yeah," he calls to everyone in and out of earshot, spinning there in the middle of the highway, "oh yeah! Explain *that*," gesturing at the two towers.

Did they just appear out of the thin

air into which things don't just disappear? It's midafternoon, hundreds of cars and trucks already having passed this way since daybreak; Aaron has driven this highway many times, as recently as the previous weekend, spotting nothing but the forbidding Badlands horizon utterly undisturbed by human endeavor. But before his eyes now, striped by their four horizontal black bands, patterned by their gray verticals—demarcating windows narrow enough to offset the absurd fear of heights felt by the Japanese-American architect who designed the structures to be the tallest that ever stood—twin towers rise from the volcanic gorge.

They aren't just the tallest things that Aaron has seen, since he knows that wouldn't be saying much. They're the tallest things most people have seen, with their two hundred twenty floors between them, each of identical height, except one is topped by a colossal aerial antenna jutting out another four hundred feet. The dual monoliths rocket to the heavens even as they're ominously earthbound. Aaron lifts the cell back to his ear. "Cee?" he says as calmly as he can manage.

Anyone who's looked at a television or the Internet or a history book the previous score of years recognizes the buildings instantly. On the other end of the phone she finally says, "I don't get it."

Some slight hysteria rises in his voice. "What do you mean you don't get it?" *Let's not fight about this too*, he thinks. "You don't see it? Them?"

"I do see it. Them. But . . . where are you?"

"Highway 44 in the Badlands. Same 44, same Badlands I drive almost every damn day."

She says, "Maybe they're a monument of some kind. . . ."

"A monument?" Aaron practically shouts in disbelief.

"Like Mount Rushmore . . ." but she understands, as he does, that having a fight about this doesn't make sense. "Okay," he snaps, "they're a monument," realizing this time he's about to hang up on her. "Don't go," she pleads, and then Aaron can hear she's scared, and knows he's scared; he peers around at the rapidly swelling sea of human disbelief, the highway traffic jam devolving to a parking lot. "They look just like in the pictures," she says.

She says, "But it can't be *them*, the actual . . . I was seventeen when they came down." It was a Tuesday, she remembers. "I mean, where did they come from? What are they doing in South Dakota?"

"What are they doing *anywhere*?" answers Aaron. He had just turned twenty-one. That weekend his pals were taking him out to get him hammered; they wound up not going. He pulls the cell from his ear for a moment to make out something, raises the phone in the Towers' direction. "Do you hear that?"

"Just your radio."

"My truck radio's not on now, and the CB is broken. It's coming from . . ." He hums to himself, trying to identify it. "What is that, anyway?" He can't tell whether the music is actually from the Towers themselves or from the earth around them.

"I think I recognize it," she says.

"You know me and music."

"One of our parents' songs," she says, "or grandparents'. . . ." She starts humming too.

"Yeah. That one." *Wait*, he thinks: *I do know this.*

". . . *address unknown* . . . ," she sings.

". . . *no such number* . . . ," he chimes in.

". . . *no such zone.*"

Or maybe they hear no such thing. It's not actually a melody, and it has no lyrics other than what they sing themselves. The "music" rises from out of or around the Towers "like the northern lights," others will say later, maybe even Aaron to Cilla Ann: "Don't the northern lights make some kind of sound?"—like a song of the spheres. When the people start coming, first by the hundreds and then the thousands, and then by the tens of thousands, from hundreds and then thousands of miles, from all over the country and then all over the continent and then all over the world, some hear the music and some don't. Some hear it take shape as a recognizable melody, some hear only a mass of harmonics.

As the crowds arrive over the following days, the families and loners, the footloose and motor-bound, the drivers and passengers and hitchhikers, the cars and RVs and trailers, the shuttles and buses and private jets, the news vans and military jeeps and airborne surveillance, the constituents and pols and advance teams, the graphic designers and Hollywood scouts and novelists who can't make up anything anymore, the mystics and cynics and the juries-still-out, the Towers loom from the end of what becomes a long national boulevard.

Drawing closer to view, the constructions of steel and tubing rise from the ground against the azurescape of the sky not as if placed there but rather as the Badlands' two most enormous buttes, shadow stalagmites of the most possessed geography of a possessed country: skywardly launched tombstones of a lakota mass grave. What once surrounded the Towers is gone. The customs office that stood at Vesey and West, the small bank once at Liberty and Church, the Marriott, and the underground mall where, on that doomsday twenty years ago, a funnel of fire flashed down ninety floors of elevator chutes before exploding into the concourse and sending thousands of morning pedestrians fleeing in panic past the boutiques and eyeglass vendors, newsstands and ATMs, the bookstore at one corner and the music shop with the flower stall behind it at the other corner across from the South Tower, past the entrances to the uptown Manhattan subway and trains to the river's Jersey side. When the sprinkler system burst, a small tidal wave swept everyone along. On that day, the people at the Towers' bottom had a more immediate sense of what was happening than those at the top where it happened. But on this day here in the Badlands, all that's left is the Towers themselves and the wind that has gusted through, and the granite and dirt at their massive forty-thousand-square-foot bases now piled in some places as high as the structures' third level, like hardened black wax holding two candles erect.

AMERICAN STONEHENGE blares the cover of one newsweekly. To some who gather, the Towers represent a hallowing of the ground. To others, particularly those who lost someone in the Towers twenty years ago, they represent a desecration. Some descendants of those who perished come to the Towers immediately, while some keep their distance, watching TVs and computers from thousands of miles away, watching for the slightest sign of life, the slightest sign that those who were in the Towers on that day are now as present as the Towers themselves.

Otherwise, media is reduced to silence as the story ends where it begins, at the Towers' edge, unless someone—soldier, adventurer, statesman, anarchist, the indignantly erstwhile or errantly intrepid—should take it upon himself to breach the periphery. But no one breaches either of the buildings. Occasional demands from some quarters that the president should enter clash with counter-demands that she shouldn't. Everyone simply bears witness to the twin ghosts and whatever three thousand human ghosts haunt it.

In silence and from a distance, the gathering listens as much as it watches. In the vacuum of what can be scientifically explained or sociologically defined, the music of the buildings provides the only explanation or definition of what has happened. The Patterson family of four from Virginia hears rising from the buildings "Oh Shenandoah," once the name—derived from the Oneida word for the antlers of a deer—of an Iroquois chief whose daughter fell in love with a white explorer.

The great national metamorphosis-song, originally a musical news bulletin from the American future, sent back to the rest of the nineteenth century by fortune hunters from across the wide Missouri, "Oh Shenandoah" is a hundred songs in one depending on who has sung or heard it at a given moment over the past two hundred years: pioneer song, sailing song, slave song, Confederate song, a French trader's love song for his Indian bride.

Older married couple Traci and Linda hear what they'll only later identify—recognizing it from a jukebox in a diner on the way back to their cottage in Upper Saskatchewan—as a ballad called "Round Midnight," not one of the accepted renditions by any number of renowned jazz giants but rather a more obscure interpretation by a 1950s San Berdoo bombshell, the daughter of vaudevillians, who took as her nom de chanson a far European capital where she never expected to sing.

Traveling from their Salt Lake City suburb home, the Mormon Hartmans (all seven) all hear (or at least six, the ten-month-old demurring from consensus) "Ecstasy of Gold," a dramatic and ghostly choral piece by a composer of Italian Western scores, while the young Ortizes—after a furious war between them over where to spend their honeymoon, with Arturo winning the last skirmish of their marriage that he ever will—pick out the strains of an early-forties composition called "Moon Mist." Very much of her time and place, Elena has never heard of Duke Ellington.

Terminally ill Justin Farber, sixty-three going on sixty-four and keenly aware he'll never stalk sixty-five, accompanied only by a jackahuahua dachshund that he named Endgame three years ago when he still thought he could be cavalier about such concepts, hears for the first time in his life a song called "Burning Airlines Give You So Much More," by a onetime seventies British glam-rocker turned ambient pioneer. A modern and sophisticated Sunni family from Egypt, the Nours, spend several days on the Internet to determine that what they've heard is "Lost Highway" by a long-dead country star; they're amused, though perhaps make too much of the synchronicity, to meet staying in the same motel the Ramseys from Tennessee trying to figure out that what they've heard is a piece—by a Nile-born woman considered the greatest Arabic singer who ever lived—called "Al-Atlal," which translates into English as "the ruins." The first lawful authority dispatched to the scene of the Towers, Sheriff Rae Jardin, hears a whistle she can't identify that fills her with dread, an old Delta blues song whose title she's never known.

In their silver Toyota Camry, a twenty-three-year-old white brother and his fifteen-year-old black sister set out from Los Angeles with no intention of driving anywhere but the shores of Lake Michigan to visit their mother, hearing only the songs— left strewn on the roadside behind them—of their father's old playlists.

Enough people report hearing music that collective psychosis can't be discounted, with the sounds in every head a kind of sonic vision or aural rorschach. Helicopters arriving within minutes of the Towers' first appearance warily circle the structures, determining that not only are there no waves of music but no waves of any natural sound whatsoever. In fact all data and instrumentation indicate that the two structures emit no vibration or frequency, not only enveloped by silence but absorbing every vibration and frequency within their proximity.

This creates not so much a black hole as what scientists soon label a "hush vortex," a misnomer since even a hush has a kind of auditory presence that collapses within the buildings' airspace. But as the white brother and his black sister from Los Angeles make the long advance in their silver Camry to their mother in Michigan, like Traci and Linda, like Justin and the Pattersons, like the Hartmans and Ortizes and Nours and Ramseys and the hundreds and then thousands and then tens of thousands of others, they're drawn to the vortex of the Badlands hush, silence descending on them with the horizon.

On the Towers' third day, an aerial photograph from one of the circling news helicopters records an image of what appears to be someone in a narrow vertical window of one of the South Tower's top floors. The image and its implications are immediately discounted by government officials as an ambiguous shadow of nothing, a trick of light. As news stations pore over the image and analyze it ceaselessly during the hours that follow, the image of someone living on one of the high floors becomes characterized as a "Turin effect," the shroud of the Tower imprinted with a vision in which people are either desperate or afraid to believe.

Enlarged, decoded, in-zoomed and out-zoomed, the photo is digitally extrapolated and reassessed from every conceivable angle and perspective. An intelligence leak reveals that in fact some within the analytic community are not at all sure they share the government's official position discounting the image. The earliest footage of the Towers is reviewed again on the theory that somebody unnoticed entered the buildings on their initial manifestation, whenever that exactly was. Descendants of those victims of the Towers' collapse on that fateful September morning demand a more convincing account either for or against the image's existence and source.

Defense surveillance, intensive media coverage, and the focus of a million amateur photographers relentlessly scour the upper floors of the South Tower for another glimpse of its occupant. As more hours pass and no further indication of life in the building presents itself, slowly but with emerging unanimity the consensus conclusion is accepted—by some with regret and by others with relief—that no one is there.

When Jesse Garon Presley wakes on the South Tower's ninety-third floor, in his first conscious moment—not a full moment; a sliver of a moment—lying there on the conference table he sees it out of the corner of his eye, right outside the northern windows: a monstrous Boeing 767 airliner flying straight toward him like a silver sun, roaring leviathan of death faster than can be comprehended, because once Jesse has comprehended what he sees, then it's gone, and he has no reason to believe he saw it at all.

Damned if Jesse has the slightest idea where he is. He closes his eyes at the sight of the plane outside the ninety-third-floor windows, and when several seconds pass and he hasn't gone up in a fireball, he opens his eyes again and the plane isn't there and he's sure he dreamed it. He sits up uneasily, dizzy, body aching. *What the hell, like I been sleeping on a damn tombstone or somethin'*, by which he means the conference table around which a couple of dozen desks fill the abandoned office space of the ninety-third floor, *and I'm not ready*, he insists to himself, *to start asking other stuff, like what is this place and how did I get here and, oh yeah, who the tarnation am I. That last one in particular, sir.*

Not so long from now he'll recall his name. But first he unbends himself from his sleep, if sleep is what it was. He lowers himself to the floor, wandering the aisles among the desks, aimlessly picking up several telephones out of nervous compulsion before actually raising one to his ear to find the line dead. The next phone on the next desk is dead too, and the phone after and all the damn phones, sir. He looks out the windows again where he dreamed he saw the plane, and as the afternoon sun sinks over the distant curve of the earth and hits the glass a certain way, he catches a reflection of himself.

He says, "Well, you *are* a good-looking rascal then," satisfied sneer curling, pointing at himself and striking a pose. But he can't pull it off, it's not *his* pose. *Since my baby left me, I found a new place to dwell* sings in his head in what he first believes is his own voice—but when he repeats it out loud, he can't pull that off either. He can't carry a tune to save his life, or to even claim his life as his own. "All right then," he says, "so I *can't* sing—whoever said I could?" and then the voice in his head answers with power, conviction, in key and with perfect pitch, *It's down at the end of lonely street*, the voice in his head that's his but isn't; and Jesse barely registers that his madness is just beginning.

The Tower is defiant in its lack of functionality, excluding the function of its own standing. Alarmed by the dry pipes in the Tower sinks, Jesse finally stumbles on an emergency room of bottled water and canned goods, part of what once was, as best he can determine, a government-related agricultural agency. No electricity works, no lights or heat or air-conditioning, with the lone exception of a small transistor radio running on batteries that he finds in one of the desk drawers. He has to remind himself what a transistor radio is. When he turns it on, he gets static. Sometimes stray bits of a tune play back.

Nothing else about the building betrays disruption. There's no rubble or disarray, everything in its place, desks tidy with paperwork and framed photos of long-ago families in other parts of the world, Europe, Asia, South America. Back on the floor where he first woke, with its rows of desks and chairs segmented into semi-cubicles and a glassed-off meeting room, the office appears to have belonged to an international "risk management" firm. He has no idea what this means or what risk the firm managed, apparently having failed to manage the biggest risk of all. At one of the desks is a woman's portrait signed *to Anthony, with love, your Pamela.*

Jesse says, "Well, Pamela darlin', I near feel now like we've met, and if ever I do get my poor self out of here, maybe I'll look you up sometime, what do you think of that?" without any way of knowing that in the twenty years since the Towers fell, Pamela has died of ovarian cancer, something she cruelly and irrationally concluded she deserved. On that September day, she heard the news of the Towers at the end of what was a long lunch hour in London, during which she had just concluded a tryst with a male lover she had been seeing and another woman she just met, a Chinese-born artist married to a professor at Kingston University, where Pamela worked in human resources.

Pamela had just gotten in the cab after leaving the hotel room when the driver told her what happened in New York. Frantically and repeatedly for the next thirty-six hours she dialed her husband before accepting what she knew was true the moment she heard the news. Over the days and weeks to come, over the months and years, she would fold her arms around her as if to hold in some part of herself. When the grief waned but not the guilt, Pamela found herself turning not to the illicit boyfriend, whom she would see again only once, but the Asian artist, for whom the dynamic of the ménage à trois unfolded exactly as anticipated. The relationship between Pamela and the other woman, such as it was, eventually ended in the wee hours one night when the artist confessed that, during the subsequent months, she watched over and over the footage of the planes exploding into the buildings because she couldn't help finding it beautiful. An American, Pamela had met Anthony in New York, returning with him to London, where he then was assigned by his company back to the Manhattan branch on a semipermanent basis; it was by an odd twist that Anthony and Pamela switched countries in their long-distance marriage. One of the last things that occurred to Pamela before she died was that she probably loved Anthony most on the night they first met, when she couldn't help falling in love as they danced to a song called "Can't Help Falling in Love."

Having vaguely realized how high ninety-three floors is, Jesse finally stops watching his own reflection in the Tower windows long enough to cast his gaze to the dakota desolation beyond. In the far distance of the craggy moonscape, so small it might be a flea crawling on the other side of the glass if fleas flew this high, he sees what he can't possibly discern is a red truck with gold racing stripes belonging to a man named Aaron, which by happenstance was the middle name—minus an *a*—of Jesse's stillborn twin brother.

A few hours later, still alone inside the Tower, from the high, dark, and narrowly vertical windows Jesse peers at the masses mobilizing on the chasm's far ridge. It's not so much a crowd that he sees, because from ninety-three floors up, there can be no such thing as a "crowd," which allows for some perception of individuals. No singular person can be seen from ninety-three floors, just as no one below might possibly glimpse Jesse a thousand feet high.

The extending multitudes outside his window form a mass that only after a while can finally be recognized as people. No hand raised in hello can be seen from where Jesse is, just as no one below can see him wave to them, as he does now and then. *Who are they and what do they want?* he wonders, as they might wonder about him in return, he figures, if they had any idea he was there.

Lying belly-down on the conference table where he first woke, chin resting on his fists, he says, "Well, I don't rightly reckon what to make of it all." From time to time he continues talking out loud like this over the next couple of days, never sure whom he addresses; he's not certain he can precisely say he's talking to himself, since he has no idea who that is. "Aaughhh!" he shouts at the singing in his head *that won't . . . shut . . . up* even in his sleep. He clasps his hands to his ears.

The voice. The voice in his head. The voice rising from the half of his id that's missing, that half's small fetal shell curled in an old shoe box on the kitchen table beside the bed where Jesse's mother gave birth to her twin sons. Wolf's purr and wildcat moan, the voice croons at Jesse (*have you heard the news?*), declares its petition and demands its tariff, siren-calling in harem chants and banshee hymnals and cowboy canticles (*blue moon, you saw me standing alone*), shuddering somewhere between genders and beyond years. The voice fills with its own echo and disputes all claims on it by either black or white. It razes artifices of progress and levels the confines of banal decades (*caught in a trap, I can't walk out*), announces the onslaught of appetite and desire (*like a river flows surely to the sea*) and the sibling reunion of God and Satan (*is what I'm now praying for*). The voice predates its own death, casts its own shadow in ecclesiastic serenades and hermaphrodite cradlesongs; it plunders the restraints of eternity. It insists on *fun*, at only the cost of Jesse's existence.

After a couple of days, Jesse attempts escape. He moves from floor to floor, trying to get out of the Tower where his wandering doesn't stop, and out of his head where the singing never ceases. He holds the fleeting hope that maybe it's the Tower that's singing to him, and that if he can flee the premises, he'll escape the voice as well. But even with his hands over his ears he can't keep out the sound, and none of the elevators run to the bottom. Prying open one of the doors of the shaft at the building's center . . .

. . . he finds himself gazing down fifteen floors to the seventy-eighth, where the Tower's occupants once changed to another elevator to the forty-fourth, where they changed again. He takes the stairs, also at the building's core, to find the doors at each level locked; the farther he descends, the louder the singing in his head grows. He reaches as far as floor sixty-seven when the prospect occurs to him that he'll get all the way to the bottom and, unable to get out—and somehow unable to get all the way back up to the only floor open to him—he'll be forever trapped in the stairwell.

the voice that is really another voice

He knows it's not really the Tower singing to him. Although the
voice in his head never stops, sometimes it sings low enough that
he almost can tune it out. Sometimes it only hums. It would be
one thing if the voice in fact was his, another if his head in fact
was someone else's. But the voice in his head is both his and not,
and that's what he can barely stand: the abel-voice in his cain-
head. It's a voice that reminds Jesse he exists in someone else's
place, a freak of fate.

When he sees, from his northern windows, the other Tower staring back at him like a mirror across the gulf, it occurs to him that
maybe *he* is over there, looking back. Momentarily he comforts
himself with the idea that *he* is over there going as mad from the
idea of Jesse as Jesse is from the idea of him. But almost as immediately he knows better, he knows there is no other, that Jesse is
alone in the place of both, that in fact the whole point of the other
Tower, the whole reason the other Tower exists, is its emptiness.

He insists out loud, "Well hell, I can too sing if I really try!" and why shouldn't it be so, if the voice singing in Jesse's head is the exact duplicate of *his*, as he keeps trying to convince himself even in the dream that he has on the third night, sleeping on the long conference table—although he couldn't have remembered what she looked like before he saw her. With his first glance, however, he recognizes immediately the woman who answers.

"You could *never* sing like that," the woman in a plain poor robe bitterly insists, suddenly standing before him. Her hair is pulled back, parted slightly on the left side—the way she often wore it, he recalls now. Her face is more handsome than lovely; his father's features actually were finer. The dirty ripped robe hangs open from her naked body and her thighs are awash with blood. She cradles something in one arm that he can't make out. In Jesse's dream so real, among the desks and cubicles surrounding where she stands, she appears to him in what he knows is a younger self, twenty-two years old (constantly shaving years off her age for the sake of her husband four years her junior), so young he barely can believe she ever was a mother at all, let alone his.

She says, "Only *he* could sing like that," holding on to one of the desks to prop herself up, "and you ain't nothing but the shadow-born that did precede him"—and with a horrified start, watching the carnage run down her thighs, making inventory of the bloody bundle she holds in the other arm, he realizes that this is the moment just after she's given birth.

"Mama?"

"You was supposed to take care of him, Jesse. You was supposed to take care of your baby brother," she says, summoning what bristling calm she can. "You was first. You was the oldest."

"Mama," he pleads, "by only half an hour!"

"In for half an hour, in for a lifetime," she says, and he has no idea what that can possibly mean.

"Only just had been born myself," he begs, "a newbie no more or less than him 'ceptin' all of thirty-some minutes—how could I have helped? How could I help him out of a womb I just left my own self?"

"If anyone should have lived," she seethes, "it was him. If you had watched out for him like a *real* big brother, it would have been him. Do you think *all them* out there"—letting go of the desk and teetering where she stands long enough to point behind her at the thousands of glittering torchlights beyond the window, stretched so far in the distant night that at the darkest and most unseen horizon the fires give way to stars—"was waiting for *you*?

Oh sure, you look like him." She pulls together both arms to secure the bloody thing she's holding. "I suppose when you talk, yes it's his voice. I suppose there's a manner or two of his you have. But though you have his same look, you don't have his same *beauty*, that beauty that's more than a face . . . you don't have the same angel-snarl. Though you have his voice, you don't have his song. You are your father's son, but *he* was *mine*, and I'm sorry but it weren't intended to be you who made it, no"—she raises the stillborn twin she's holding—"it was supposed to be him."

He cries, "Oh, Mama, don't," clasping his ears and closing his eyes, the vision of his mother unleashing a flood of waking memories. The move to Memphis. The year his daddy went to jail for altering a paycheck. The small public-housing unit like a palace compared to the two-room shack with no plumbing where he was born, his stillborn twin lying in the shoe box on the kitchen table, his mother crying all night that it couldn't have been Jesse she lost instead. His twin brother's shabby little grave back in Tupelo at Priceville Cemetery, where Jesse watched his piss soak the sheltering earth and imagined it staining the infant bones.

He remembers the Sunday mornings when his mother tried to drag him to church, Jesse rejecting any part of it. The times when he took God's name in vain to offend not only her but the memory of *him*, as though to profane into nothingness whatever sacred memory anyone could have of him. Humes High in Memphis, where, king stud of the corridors, Jesse cut his sexual swath through the school's female population to show what they would have missed had they squandered on *him* their moans and swoons. Where, as his father's son, he wrought terror on every mama's boy he could grab from every classroom and hallway and roadside up to Poplar Avenue.

Down at the paint plant on the afternoon he was expelled from school, young Jesse told his father, "No one wants me here," expecting his daddy would, as usual, answer nothing.

"I know," said Vernon. "Exceptin' me."

"All of them," said Jesse, turning to look at the shadow the sun cast behind him that wasn't his, "are going to make me pay for not being him."

His father answers, "I know, boy. They gonna make you pay forever . . ." and Jesse wakes himself, wondering how he could deserve such a nightmare.

Up he staggers from the conference table to where she stood in his "dream." On the carpet, he finds blood's unmistakable sign, wonders if the stain was there all along and if his vision of her grew from it. But he knows better when the singing starts again. *I was the one who taught her to cry when she wants you under her spell*, and Jesse nearly takes a letter opener from one of the desks and plunges it through his ear into his brain to cut the sound out. Hurling himself headlong into the window, he hopes to shatter it, if not himself. But he's not a United flight 175 en route from Boston to Los Angeles; bounced off the window, Jesse crumples into a heap in the corner.

Train I ride, sixteen coaches long.

A quarter of a mile below and eight hundred miles away, fifteen-year-old Zema and twenty-three-year-old Parker are pulling out of Flagstaff onto Interstate 40 in their silver Camry when she reads the news on her cell phone. "The Twin Towers," she informs her brother, "just showed up in South Dakota."

Unlike the Ramseys and Nours and Ortizes and Hartmans and Pattersons, unlike Justin and Linda and Traci, Zema and Parker haven't set out on their journey for the purpose of going to the Badlands. On their way from L.A. to Lake Michigan to see their mother, the siblings intend to drive old Route 66 cross-country from its origin at the now-desolate Santa Monica Pier.

. . . plays the car stereo now, a song their parents used to listen to, their father preferring the version by a black forties piano player while their mother favored the one by a white sixties band from London. Either way, Parker now contemplates ruefully, whenever any of the hip-hop artists *he* used to listen to rapped about getting *their* kicks, the oldsters were less enthralled. Driving Route 66 together as a family was once their mother's dream, because she always loved the story of Route 66.

Having been stopped at the California border, however, with the sandstorms of L.A. rising in the rearview mirror and their trunkful of contraband water seized by border guards, the siblings have abandoned the route. Parker says, "Don't tell Mom," and in rare accord with her brother as they skirt the southern vicinity of the Grand Canyon, Zema reads her phone. "Did you hear what I said?" she asks. He turns up the music in the car and she turns it back down. "All right," Parker answers testily, "the Twin Towers just showed up in South Dakota."

She cries, "Oh my God, we've got another two thousand miles, let's not start!"

"So," he says, voicing the thing that's been nagging him, "are we going to run into what we did last night every time we try to find a motel to stay?"

"That was my fault?" When he doesn't answer, she sits up in the passenger seat and repeats, "Wait. That was *my* fault?"

"I didn't say that." He glances over at her.

"Watch the road."

"Did I say that?"

"Would you please watch the road?"

"I am watching the road."

"You're not."

After a pause he says, "Are we going to have to get two rooms every night? We'll be broke before we're halfway." When the motel in Flagstaff refused them a single room, hair-trigger Parker almost lunged at the owner behind the front desk as Zema pulled him back. "A little fucking twentieth-century, isn't it?" Parker exploded at the motel manager, who shouted back something about transporting underage girls across the state line, pointing indignantly at Zema. Parker wanted to break off the man's finger. Only when his sister got Parker outside did it hit him. "Underage?" he said, looking at her in confusion.

Zema said, "Don't you get it? It's not a race thing," and the horror on Parker's face might have made her laugh if she hadn't felt as mortified. "Well, we don't exactly look like brother and sister," she reasoned.

Parker considered this a moment before announcing, "That's the most disgusting thing I've ever heard."

"Likewise, dude. Let's just go on to the next place, okay?"

But at the next place they still wound up taking two rooms. That Zema has assumed her mother's last name on her student ID and Parker his father's on his driver's license hardly makes less complicated that she's black and he's white. "Why didn't you just keep Dad's name?" Parker complains outside Winslow behind the wheel of the car. "You used it all the way through seventh grade or whenever it was."

"I like Mom's name," Zema answers quietly, and then, "Not like I'm choosing Mom over Dad."

She says, "Where is South Dakota anyway?"

"Why are we going to—?"

"The *Twin Towers*," she says, shoving the phone at him, "look."

"Uh, trying to drive here. . . ."

"*Look*." She holds the phone in front of his face and he swats it away. "Jesus, Sheba!" he cries, before correcting himself— "Zema"—under his breath. For years after they adopted her from Ethiopia at the age of two, the family called her Sheba, as in Queen of, a thousand years BC. Now to compound the confusion of last names, Parker's sister has taken on her given Amharic birth name . . . *so how are we supposed to keep straight what to call her?* fumes Parker.

If at least she kept the same last name, we might be able to get one fucking motel room together, he thinks. Zema persists with the phone and he grabs it from her and looks, swerving. She shouts, "Watch the road!"

"You're the one shoving your fucking phone in my face!" He says to the phone with a glance, "Okay, I see it. Yup, looks just like the Twin Towers."

"They don't know if they're the *actual* Twin Towers or . . ."

"Well they can't be the actual Twin Towers," he replies, "can they? Believe me, I saw them come down."

He didn't really see them come down, but it's something he can hold over her, since it took place five years before she was born. He was three, in the canyon outside L.A. where they lived; his parents kept him home from school that day, like all the other parents. In the hours afterward, the whole country thought planes were falling from the sky. He wasn't allowed to watch television, and for years after Zema came, their father wouldn't let her watch footage of it until she finally pulled it up on YouTube when he wasn't around.

Now, in the car, Parker forgets about the Towers until he messages his girlfriend—who recently entered a rehab center in Vancouver, putting their relationship to the test—and her only answer asks if he's seen the news. Brother and sister grab sandwiches off the highway to Albuquerque, where they hope to spend the night. "So far they're identical to the actual Towers," she says, sipping her Coke.

"Who says?" answers Parker. "I don't know what that even means."

"Me neither," agrees Zema. She declares, "We're going," and Parker shakes his head—*just like Mom*—smiling a bit at the memory of their father, who always told Parker that if anyone was like his mother, it was her son.

bar code

In black letters against the gray outer walls, a motel west of Albuquerque identifies itself: MOTEL. So generic, muses Parker, "I'm surprised it doesn't have a bar code next to it." He and Zema study the letters through the car's windshield; the art student/conceptualist in Parker likes the idea of the bar code and suppresses the impulse to tag the motel with one, his tagging days having ended when he was Zema's age and arrested by a sheriff for spray-painting canyon rocks.

In the motel's registration "office," Zema takes charge, as she figures she probably should have back in Flagstaff. "He's my brother," she confidently explains to the Native American woman behind the counter. The woman looks at the teenage girl, at Parker, back at Zema, and says, "Okay." Parker interjects, "She took our mom's name, we used to both have our dad's but—" but the woman waves this away and Zema says, "Parker, she said okay. She believes us."

"Or doesn't give a shit," the young man mutters.

"Hey." The woman behind the counter fixes him with a stare. "I believe you."

Parker lets his sister have the single bed. On the floor he piles towels from the bathroom and an extra blanket from the room's closet. The two have take-out Mexican for dinner, then with his institutionalized girlfriend in Vancouver the brother texts himself into unconsciousness, as Zema lies on her bed watching the nineteen-inch television. She has flipped through all eight channels a couple of times before settling on the news station broadcasting—in Spanish she doesn't understand—the story of the Towers in the Badlands and the hundreds of thousands of people descending.

With the light off and Parker snoring on the floor, Zema looks out the window beside her bed and makes out in the dark a large dead oak and low stone wall beyond it, cacti beyond that, desert wind rattling the sagebrush. Although she realizes the next morning that it must have been a dream, she watches in the night an exodus of displaced Navajos as far as the eye can see, marching past the motel by the hundreds, braves and their women and children at the gunpoint of soldiers on horseback.

When she wakes to sunlight, she repeats flatly to the window what she said in the car the day before, "We're going," figuring her brother—curled beside her among the bath towels—is still sleeping. "You said that yesterday," he answers from the floor.

Neither is much for maps. After punching "Michigan" into his cell back in L.A. and assuming the device would talk them through the next two thousand miles, now Parker has the revelation that looking at an actual map might approximate the psychological sensation of knowing where they are. This takes on more significance when they're no longer sure where they'll sleep.

Parker tosses aside the towels and blankets on which he's spent the night and spreads across the floor the map they got at a convenience store in Kingman. He crawls around it several times before he's sure, more or less, that he and the map are aligned and pointing the same direction.

Determining Albuquerque is in New Mexico is one thing. But now, studying the map—and in part because, even fifteen hundred miles away, he's disinclined to give his mother the satisfaction of being right—Parker withholds from his sister larger concerns, born of paying just enough attention to the news to know that between here and Michigan is more trouble than roads and routes and maps can resolve.

What Parker hasn't told Zema is that after all those years when their mother wanted that big Route 66 road trip, now, if it were up to her, they wouldn't be driving at all. On Interstate 40 through northeast Arizona and the western part of New Mexico, the brother and sister already have passed signs of the Rupture, banners of Disunion flying from flagpoles and fastened to the few bare trees that defy the desert rock. Until she finally looks back up at him across the map there in the Bar Code Motel, Parker studies his sister.

Silently he stews over territorial frontiers yet to be crossed. He stews over border guards yet to be answered to, and Rupture zones all over Kansas, Oklahoma, Texas, where the siblings need to pick up Route 83 in the Panhandle past Amarillo and head almost due north for South Dakota—or as best as Parker can determine, anyway, given that he hasn't any more forbearance for figuring out such things than anyone else born within the temporal radius of the twenty-first century. "Dad always said no one in this family has the slightest patience," Parker muses, expecting nothing from Zema, who, notwithstanding the old playlists on the car stereo, rarely responds to mention of their father. So it's a surprise when she mutters in return, "As though he did."

Parker was also surprised at the trip's outset when Zema downloaded their father's playlist onto the car stereo. This was after trying to find a radio station in the fourteen-year-old Camry with two hundred thousand miles on it that Parker inherited to no objection from Zema, who usually protested on sheer principle whenever her brother was favored for anything and any reason.

Shooting her a sideways look, he had said it as casually as possible, "Dad's playlist." When Zema didn't answer, he pressed, "Remember he always wanted to upgrade the sound system in this thing? We were always on him about his boring mu—"

"I remember," she had snapped. Now, as they cross Navajo and Acoma lands, a song from the playlist called "Little Sister" comes on the stereo. Parker turns it off. "Don't need any songs about little sisters, thank you," he tells his little sister.

"He's not singing about *his* little sister," she explains, "he's singing about—"

"I know what he's singing about," says Parker, slightly stunned when Zema shoots back, "Dad loved this guy," the first declamatory thing about their father that he can remember her saying in years.

Although he doesn't want to discourage it, he can't help answering, "*You* loved this guy."

"What?"

"You loved this guy," he is adamant.

"Uh, I . . ." but even Zema knows her dissent sounds hesitant.

"First it was Mr. English Spaceguy with the red hair who wore dresses," Parker says, "then it was *him*," pointing at the stereo. "Dad *liked* him, *you* loved him."

Parker thinks it's typical that the first conversation they've had about their father in as long as he can remember, they're arguing about his music. "What Dad loved," Parker continues, "was all that sixties shit that doesn't make sense. The walrus one and—"

"Walrus?"

"The point is, Dad *liked* him well enough," he says, gesturing once more at the singer on the stereo, "but *you* had him on your bedroom wall. You had the birthday party with all his songs. Out went the Jean Genies and in came the hound dogs. You were crushing on his cheekbones when you were seven, before you went all blackedy-black on us."

Zema looks at him. "Excuse me?"

"Never mind," he answers.

"Wait—"

"I didn't mean anything by it," Parker insists irritably, "forget it, I take it back. Fuck," he mutters, "I was blacker than you were." Neither can remember their ever having had a conversation like this, but then they haven't ever had a real conversation about much of anything.

She does vaguely recall a poster on her wall when she was eight: the singer as a cowboy drawing a six-gun from his holster as though in a gunfight in a Western, no cowboy hat, long-sleeve buttoned shirt and boots and jeans double-belted. The image duplicated, looking not square into the camera but ever so slightly off right.

That was about the time when her sense of racial identity began to take hold. When she learned of black baseball players in the forties from biopics that their father took her to see, African-American ministers shot down. It was about the time she became more aware of herself as a black girl, their mother quizzing her as to who was singing on the radio. "This?"

"Billie Holiday," Zema would answer.

"This?"

"Aretha."

Soon, as Parker might put it, out went *I'm all shook up* and in came *I break out in a cold sweat.* As the cultural paradox of the times would have it, she *did* first learn her blackedy-black from her white hip-hop brother, remembering now something their father told Parker the time they were all stranded in London, one night when both father and son thought she was asleep. In the next room her father talked to her brother—younger then than Zema is now—like she had never heard, his voice taking on an uncommon urgency. "You can't use that word," he said, "it's the worst word you can use. I'd rather you use the F-word, not that I want you to use it either. But better that. I know they use it in the music you listen to, but language exists in a context, and if they use that word among themselves, it means something different than if you use it, do you understand?"

"I've never used it," she heard her brother.

"I know that," their father answered, "but I'm telling you anyway. It's important you understand. *You* use that word and it means four hundred years of terrible shit whether you mean it or not. So I don't want to hear it from you and I don't want your sister to hear it. She'll hear it too soon enough, but not from anyone in this family."

"All right," Parker answered quietly, trying to muster some rebellious irritation with little success, and Zema wanted to jump up and run into the next room and defend him.

Because Zema has a secret: she adores him. Although she'll go to extraordinary lengths to dispute it, she adores Parker even more than she adores her mother and even more than her father, whenever she can bring herself to think of her father. When she was two and her mother came to get her from the orphanage in Addis Ababa, among all the gifts and mementos it was Parker's photo that the girl clutched in her hand and wouldn't let go, even if subsequent years might have found sister and brother barely on speaking terms, except when she was provoking him or he was insulting her.

At the depths of their relationship, her secret adoration of him—sometimes almost secret to herself—is such that she has tried to be him. This was during the time she insisted to her family and everyone else that she was a boy, a phase that may or may not be ending now. There have been years she was confused, and more recent years when she may still have been confused or only pretending to be confused. In the thirteen years since Zema came to America, she has never had any idea that having no idea who she is and having no idea where she belongs makes her more American than anyone. For his part, Parker hasn't so much failed to acknowledge his sister's adoration as refused to. Neither has yet learned how time lays relentless siege to the denials of hearts drawn most inexorably to the truth.

Staring at her cell in the passenger seat, Zema says, "There's music coming out," and it's half a minute before Parker, distracted, barely answers, "Turn it off if you want."

She looks at her brother and then at the car stereo. "Out of the Towers, I mean," she says. On the highway they pass slashing blood-red mesas rising like octaves and tiny towns crowned by signs that announce their names from towering bluffs flanked by flags, mostly Disunion. LEVI'S FROM NEW YORK! promises one storefront. Overhead, a skywriter jet unzips the sky. "Music," she clarifies, "is coming out of the Towers."

Parker says, "What towers?"

She rolls her eyes. "The Towers we're driving four hundred miles out of our way for." She can't tell if her brother is still distracted or if distraction has given way to confusion. Finally he says, "Someone inside is playing music?"

"No one is inside," she explains, "there's music coming from them. Isn't that what I said?"

"Like, what, it's a stereo? They're big speakers or something? One's bass and the other's treble?"

"Speakers? What are you talking about? They're two buildings a hundred stories tall."

"No."

stereo (bass)

Zema says to her brother, "What do you mean no?" As they near the Texas border, I-40 turns into a so-called thruway, federal interstate protected by chain fence trespassing Rupture territories marked by more Disunion flags. Since checking out of the Bar Code Motel, Parker and Zema have heard on three different occasions of a rumored thoroughfare unmarked on any map, a secret highway called the "shadowbahn" that cuts through the heart of the country from one end to the other with impunity.

Crossing friendly Union and hostile Disunion territories alike, allegedly the secret highway runs from an undisclosed western point to an undisclosed eastern, as though there is no America at all of physicality or fact, only the America of the mind—whatever America that might be, to whatever mind might ponder it. "They're not a hundred stories tall," Parker answers.

Zema practically shouts, "They're the flippin' Twin Towers!"

"But not the real Twin Towers."

She sighs in exhaustion. "We had this conversation."

"How do you know?"

"That they're a hundred sto—?"

"That no one's inside."

Zema thinks a minute. "They would know."

"Has anyone gone inside?" says Parker.

"Of course not."

"So where is the music coming from?"

"The *Towers*."

"But what is it? This music. I mean, is it Beethoven? Wu-Tang Clan . . . ?" He laughs, pleased with himself.

"Everyone hears something different."

"So basically," he reasons, "everyone there is just going nuts." She starts to challenge this conclusion but stops. "Why hasn't anyone gone inside?" he says.

She looks at him. "No one wants to."

"Why not?"

She's still looking at him. "*Why not?*" she says so incredulously that, especially under the heat of her glare, it makes him look back at her. "Keep your eyes on the road," she says, then, "maybe *you're* a little nuts."

He looks back at the road, then looks at her again. Then he pulls the car over to the side of the highway and stops.

"What are you doing?" she says.

He turns off the ignition and twists in his seat to face her. For the first time, she finally detects in him apprehension. "Wait a minute," he says, finally getting it, voice slightly breaking. "Are you trying to tell me these are the *real* Twin Towers?"

Within two hours of the

Towers' initial sighting, Sheriff Jardin gave her deputy a hard look when he asked her the same question. Behind them, traffic on the highway gathered in full force. Around them, the crowd of onlookers billowed. The two continued watching the Towers awhile in silence until the deputy said, "You going in, then?"

The sheriff gave him another hard look. Unsettled enough by a lot more than her displeasure, the deputy dropped formalities. "Rae," he protested as respectfully as he could manage, "you gotta stop looking at me like I'm the craziest thing that's happening here."

The deputy persisted, "And I notice you didn't answer my last question."

"You noticed correctly," said the sheriff. "Damned astute of you, too."

Gazing at the rapidly escalating number of cars and people, the deputy asked, "So are, uh, we in charge here?"

"Don't know if this is even county jurisdiction." The sheriff nodded at the Towers. "Where they're standing may be tribal land."

The deputy peered the other way at a red truck with gold racing stripes. "By the way, first suspect to see the Towers, or to claim to see them, is right over th—"

The sheriff said, "Suspect?"

Jesus, she's a bitch today. Didn't take that early retirement early enough for either of us. "Okay, I guess he's not actually suspected of anything. Also—"

"*Man* you have a lot of questions, Deputy."

"And you don't? I just—"

"What?"

"—hear . . . music."

"Let's go talk to the *suspect*, shall we?" said the sheriff. "Maybe if we lock him up, all this will go away." She wished the song that was whistling in her head would go away too.

Aaron explained, "I came around the bend and there they were."

"That bend?" In her midfifties with the faintest trace of an accent, graying hair pulled back in a short ponytail, the sheriff pointed over Aaron's shoulder. "How do you know you were the first one to see them?"

"I was the only one here," Aaron told her, "then everyone stopped. Unless someone before me just drove right past without noticing."

"Ever drive this way before?"

"All the time. Sioux Falls to Rapid City." She studied his red truck with the stripes and a bumper sticker she didn't understand. Around the same bend, other law enforcement was arriving; new aerial reconnaissance circled overhead. The sheriff turned back to Aaron. "So in other words," she said, now pointing in the eastern distance, "coming down 44 from that direction, you saw nothing at all until the bend."

"That's right."

"Doesn't make much sense, does it?"

"Oh," Aaron answered a bit heatedly, "like the rest of this does." The two locked eyes. "Can I ask you something?"

"Okay."

"You do hear that, right? Music?"

"No, sir," she lied emphatically. "I don't hear anything."

The phenomenon of the Towers' reappearance two decades after their downfall is so terrifying and so eludes explanation as
to avoid lesser phenomena of society and commerce. Even as the
throngs continue to gather, no souvenir stands have appeared, no
pennants have been sold, or buttons. A few entrepreneurs have
tried to hawk sandwiches and soda, only to meet rejection and
indifference. Contention among county, state, and federal gov-
ernments as to who has domain is complicated by circumstances
in which no one knows what "domain" means.

For some, the Towers' appearance makes a mockery of their disappearance. Some "news" channels that need not be identified
suggest that the Towers are a federal conspiracy, although to what
end even excitable commentators find confounding. Others ar-
gue that the new Towers are a pernicious kind of jihadist attack,
an act of mass psychological terrorism aimed at deranging not
just a nation but a defiled century and whatever defiled world
inhabits it. To still others, the onset of End Times is so obvious as
to barely warrant its loud and incessant mentioning.

By the fourth day, several hundred thousand congregate at the Towers. They keep a distance that's been dictated by nothing other than some collective judgment to go no nearer. If anything, the impulse of the gathered throng is to pull back. They can't be said to wait, since waiting implies an expectation of something and no one has such expectation. Once the curious have observed the Towers in the same way they would the world's oldest redwood or presidents' faces carved in rock, nothing holds them but an inexplicable covenant struck between those already there and those who keep coming.

When the state attorney general lands by helicopter that afternoon, the sheriff still hears in her head the whistled tune from the Towers that she's denied since arriving. "My God, what a scene," the attorney general calls breathlessly from beneath the whap of chopper blades, "you the senior officer in charge of this investigation?"

"Is this an investigation?" she shouts back in his ear as they walk from the noise.

"You're going in," he says.

"Sorry?"

"Somebody needs to go in."

"In where?"

"In those," he says, pointing at Towers he won't name that sing a song she won't acknowledge.

The sheriff says, "Sir, I'm three and a half months from early retirement."

"A nice way," the attorney general answers, "to cap off a career, wouldn't you say?"

This son of a bitch being funny? she fumes. "Not particularly,
no."

"Your jurisdiction, Sheriff."

"Actually it's not been determined that *those* are in Penning-
ton County at all. Where they're standing may very well be Lakota land."

The attorney general's eyebrows arch. "I don't even want to
hear that. I'm not so sure the tribal council elders want to hear it
either. They certainly haven't laid any claims. In fact those Towers may be the only part of America they haven't laid claim to in
the last couple hundred years. Where are you from?"

Oh, so this is the way you guys do it, she thinks. Louisiana,
she almost answers before she says, "I'm from South Dakota, Mr.
Attorney General."

"I mean originally," as though he cares.

She repeats, "I'm from South Dakota," and I went to a lot
of damned trouble to not be from anywhere else. But now the
song in her head grows. "All right"—the attorney general's tone
changes—"now listen. Someone has to go in. We've got people

thinking they see things, crazy rumors that someone's up on the ninety-something floor—"

"I'm not going to the ninety-something floor."

"We could put you on the rooftop—"

She takes the badge off her coat lapel. "No."

"Like you were saying, Sheriff," he says coolly, "early retirement."

"I'll go in at the bottom," she says, nodding at the South Tower's entrance in the distance, "have a look around. Otherwise you can take my early retirement and shove—"

"All right, all right," waving away her threat. For a moment each regards the other in silence. "I believe," says the attorney general, with the faintest trace of a smile that the sheriff would love to stick a gun in, "the whole wide world has come to the conclusion that you're the perfect person for this job."

"I believe the whole wide world has no idea whatsoever who I am," she answers.

"Exactly."

A few hours later, as dusk begins to fall, approaching the South Tower from twenty feet the sheriff hears louder than she's heard for three days the whistling tune. Not only is she closer than she's been to the Tower from which the song comes, but the surrounding landscape has become more silent than it's been since the Towers appeared. The strangest, most extraordinary stillness falls on the multitude of what now is an estimated half million who have swarmed to the site in the past week.

Raising a hand to her eyes and squinting in the sun now setting over a distant western ridge, the sheriff stops and looks back over her shoulder at everyone watching her. Even the whir of the helicopters above seems to fall suddenly soundless. If she has lied to everyone about the song she hears in her head, she no longer can lie to herself; if she left behind almost everything about Louisiana, including most of her accent, there remains a Delta blues whistled by her grandfather when she was four, with words that go, although she's never known them, *I can tell the wind is rising, hellhound on my trail.*

But she doesn't really remember any of this yet. That memory will come crashing back in a few moments inside the South Tower lobby, which appears—in contrast to the distinctly businesslike lobby of the North Tower—like the foyer of a grand theater or cathedral. It has narrowly vertical, high-arched windows and rolling carpet as brilliant red as blood and as perfectly unblemished and untrodden as after its final vacuuming that September day twenty years ago. The golden balcony swoops around the lobby like a semitone or A-sharp.

A score of the Tower's nearly hundred elevators stretch before her. The sheriff feels silly calling, "Hello?" as though anyone would possibly answer. "Hello?" she calls again, but more quietly. If anyone were up in the Tower, wouldn't they have migrated to the bottom by now? They wouldn't remain at the top, would they? "Hello?" for the third and final time, crossing the enormous red lobby toward the song and the frosted radiance that she now can hear and see coming from the final set of elevator doors at the far end.

the beckoning (two)

It's not clear anymore to even her that it's a beckoning, or whether anyone but her is being beckoned. "No," she says now to no one, to the memory she hasn't remembered yet, and draws back in the cavernous lobby that rises a hundred feet. She looks up at the balcony, from which peer down a thousand ghosts she can't see but knows are there. Outside the lobby windows, night falls and she clicks on her flashlight; the whistled song from the glow at the far elevator doors pulls her like her grandfather pulled her along the swampland road on the other side of Lake Pontchartrain when she was four, apricot-toned cotton dress sticking to her small body . . .

. . . in the wet air, rain of the vestigial afternoon shower falling from the trees' higher leaves to the lower. Then the sound of raindrops acceded to the growing laughter of men and maybe— although she can't be sure she didn't imagine it—a single small scream. "Come on now, darlin'," her grandfather chuckled deeply, "you're about to *see* somethin'," and with the spot of her flashlight dancing before her, the sheriff finds the final pair of elevator doors parted as no others. Reaching the doors, she taps them quick as though they might be molten and she would be scorched by what's behind; she's shocked how easily they slide open. She barely has to pull the doors apart.

Come on now, darlin', you're about to see *somethin'.* She doesn't think to draw the gun from her holster; she can't imagine anything more useless. Behind the elevator doors lurks no shaft, no elevator car to carry her. Behind the doors is Another Place and Another Time that doesn't belong here any more than does the Tower, a place of her past into which she might now step and nearly does, her grandfather's whistle—of a black man's blues no less—adrift in the bayou air like a dandelion blown scattered. Her foot raised, the sheriff is poised to step across the elevator threshold . . . when she's gripped by the realization that, landing this step, she'll never return. Looking up from her withdrawn foot, confronted by the place and time she was four in Louisiana with her grandfather's hand gripping hers hard, what she hasn't remembered in half a century suddenly is vivid down to the particular blue of the sky, the particular waft of the wind, the particular caw of circling crows, the particular mob before her, laughing beneath the grand bayou oak from which hang by ropes on the lowest branch three bodies, smoke rising off them from their particular dying blazes, the smallest body belonging to what even a girl of four knows was another little girl not so much older than she, charred so black that it can't be seen she was black before burning; and a four-year-old white girl can't figure out how another little girl could possibly deserve this, other than being black before burning. Half a century from her small self, the sheriff turns and flees the red Tower, hellhounds on the trail of her country.

opens his eyes again. Lying across the conference table like it's the top of a tombstone, he opens his eyes like he did the first morning when, for a brief moment, he thought he saw a flaming airliner flying into him. He sits up, looking at the darkened building around him.

He looks around him as if something in or of the Tower itself, somewhere ninety-two floors below, has awakened him. For a while he doesn't move, face in his hands; finally he rises from the table. "All right then," he says quietly to no one.

After the dream of his mother, Jesse understands that those as-sembled outside below his windows are the enemy. He never be-lieved they were there for him; he has no earthly idea why they're out there at all. But he understands now that if they knew he was up here on the ninety-third floor, he would be the object of their hostility.

"All right then," he says again. He understands that whatever conspiracy *the other one* might have entered into with the public there beyond the window, had *he* lived rather than Jesse, isn't any of which Jesse can ever be part. This moment, like all of Jesse's moments, exists within the shadow of the other life never lived. He knows they hate him, even if they don't know he's here.

Prowling to the black window and the nation at his feet, he says, "I'm not your irresistible delinquent god, then, not your honky-tonk Amun hiding in plain sight, no. Not," he says, plastering himself to the cold black glass, "your American Hick, dixie jeremiah wreathed in laurels of some such boogie-woogie jook. I'm yer bringer of Music Death, just as y'all say, your deliverer of Rant, sir, in the black echo of which no music can endure. I come to cut low the Grand Domestic Hymn, sir. I embark to ride the mystery train of Tuneless Shout, destined for aleatoric hinterwilds beyond where timbre chokes on the color of its own tone. Here I am then!" pounding the windows, shouting at them below. "I didn't reject your music—your music rejected me. So here I am, Presley the First: Jesse Garon! the *only* fucking Presley in case y'all ain't noticed. Having beaten your beloved mama's boy to the finish line, having outraced him down Miss Gladys's fallopian express lane in a deafening dash—*deafening*—for freedom, for deliverance from the mama who spurned him. And your mama's boy? He couldn't keep the fuck up, that's what." Jesse turns his head, calls back over his shoulder, "Where you be now, little bro? How you coming now, baby brother? That's all right for you, just take your damned sweet time, *because I got here first.*"

the fill of the sky

When he hears the new song, it's not like any he's heard in his head. He needs a moment to locate it at the other end of the office space; the song cuts through the static of the transistor radio that he found in the desk drawer. It plays to Jesse direct and clear, as if provoked by the building itself, wafting out of the dark expanse of the ninety-third floor.

The song is more a broadcast of hostilities, half-wail/half-news flash dispatching bad news. A rural-nuclear dirge that's unlike any Jesse ever would have heard on the radio, let alone in his head, if he even could remember ever having heard anything on a radio. It may be that this song, by a punk tribe from Leeds relocated to the American Midwest, never has been played on any radio at all.

It's a song that announces nothing less than the Death of Song. It's music that insists on nothing more than the End of Music. Mini-soundtrack of bedlam so steeped in the age's marrow that whatever once might have been the cause of the chaos, or accepted as the cause of the chaos, reveals another preceding moment of causality, and then a moment before that and another before that. *Trouble down south*, sings the singer to a backdrop of mournful voices . . .

. . . although the south of where isn't clear. Fiddle and then other violins barely float mid-communiqué like police reports as the song threatens to come apart. *Sky fills with blades, sound falls from above. Avoid strong light* is the singer's final warning, *stay underground.* But Jesse, thrilled, rushes for the stairwell that he's descended several times to no avail. "Well, sir," he calls, flinging open the stairway door, "if there's nowhere to go down, then I'll go up."

the beckoning (three)

He says, "I'll go up, and see if all them circling choppers can ignore me then? Try to miss me then," and in the darkened stairwell
he feels the steps at his feet and climbs. He calls, "You up there,
baby brother? Mama's little girl with his little-girl lips and his
little-girl hips? Here comes the *man* of the family! shot forth
from the top of this here Tower like one last drop of mongrel jism,"
and as Jesse leaps the steps in the dark to the ninety-fourth floor,
the ninety-fifth and ninety-sixth, the song from the radio follows.

With every passing floor, the singing that's been in Jesse's head
these days grows at once fainter and more desperate. The radio's
song that he thought was on the ninety-third floor below him
now beckons from above, although it's not clear to him it's a
beckoning, or whether anyone but him is being beckoned. First
imperceptibly, then more clearly, the stairwell that Jesse hikes
glows lighter. Leaning over the rail of the steps, he cranes to
peer up.

A faint, frosted radiance at the top—the size of a single musical note—is nearly corporeal. Jesse's eyes adjust, and with every passing level the light above grows. Running out of steps at the hundred and seventh floor, he stumbles into what he barely makes out once was a food court, sandwich shops in the semidark, pasta joints, sushi eateries, posters for soda and frozen yogurt. NATHAN'S FAMOUS HOT DOGS reads a sign in the Tower's murk.

He's startled to see at the floor's far end, next to a stalled escalator ascending the remaining levels, TOP OF THE WORLD with an arrow pointing, as though it could be anything but literal. Three flights above, at the far end of the escalator, gleams the signal's source. The closer that Jesse comes, the more the frosted light grows to the size of a man. As he bounds the escalator's metal steps three, four, five at a time, Jesse nears—buried deep at the light's core—the faint outline of a memory: "Union Square," he blurts, *I believe I do recollect something . . .*

. . . and with a lurch from the static escalator's last step, he tumbles out onto the Tower's open rooftop, into a foyer of miasma and night where all noise collapses in on itself. Somewhere higher off the planet than almost anyone has walked short of the moon, Jesse has just enough time to reach above him and touch the black arched ceiling of the globe. Ever so briefly he takes in the roof's layout, centered by its railed island platform that's surrounded by an empty concrete moat and, at the far rim, a fence once placed so as to prevent jumpers, or at least anyone jumping for any reason other than oncoming aircraft.

Midair in the moment's leap from the escalator into the light, Jesse gasps. Midair in the moment's leap, he feels a gust blow him outside his twin brother's life into his own. Squinting hard into the portal of light before him, he remembers a photo shoot on Forty-Seventh Street before the studio moved to Union Square, and of course the image that he's been seeing in the light these past few minutes is of himself: two of him, side by side.

Two of him side by side—or so Jesse thought when the photographer took the double image all those years ago, wanting as the photographer always did to make the most of his superstars, the double image reproduced and silkscreened in variations of color. Both twins postured with six-gun drawn from a holster as though in a Western gunfight, no cowboy hat, long-sleeve buttoned shirt and boots and jeans double-belted with holster slung low on the right hip. Looking not square into the camera but ever so slightly off right; this image that Jesse now surveys is silver and black. But for the first time since that photo shoot decades before, Jesse realizes what he never realized, that they never were double images of him at all: "So, you and me then, baby bro," he says, staring at the identical twins glistening in the tower-rooftop portal, "it was you and me all along, huh. Never," he realizes, "was just *me* and me at all, should have known. Andy always was up to *something*, manipulative little albino twat . . . he knew all along it was you right there beside me"—and as Jesse steps through the glowing door on the Tower rooftop into Another Place and Another Time, he lapses midstep from the consciousness of one split moment into the consciousness of another.

Through his head blows a black soundless wind that, for the first time, justifies every moment of him. He barely can be sure now that he's ever been in the Tower at all. There beneath the ceiling of the world, where nothing lies in the distant dark but moonscape and the twinkling of thousands of flaming lights gathered at the Towers' base, for the first time since that original flashing glimpse outside the ninety-third-floor window of the airliner coming toward him, he's ecstatic. The Towers and their future vanish behind him, the single fiery siren-note that has beckoned him goes up in its own flames. Embers of incinerated music scatter on the rooftop from where, seconds ago, crossing a threshold similar to the one from which Sheriff Rae Jardin recoiled more than a hundred floors below, Jesse the Shadow-Born jumped and—in the eyes of anyone else who might have been on the Tower rooftop to witness it—disappeared into thin air.

two

supersonik

Day 0 Millenniux (9/12/01)
Almanac in Song, or an Autobiographical Soundtrack

as originally inventoried by Parker and Zema's
father for the fifteen-year-old girl reading it now,
America flowing past her window on the passenger
side, motel windows flickering in the dark before the
playlists' songs will sputter from not the radio but the
receiver of her body and the stereo of her eyes.

The first is a song of both morning and mourning [chronicles the father's log], beginning with a saxophone's outburst that settles into prayer before the piano's benediction. The tension lies not in whether brass or ivory will dominate the other but which will succeed in achieving oblivion—a song about what and who will be the last left standing not in victory but bleeding abandonment, envying the vanquished. Sounding to the modern Western ear something between medieval and Middle Eastern in its dissonances, the second song is a lament by Old World futurists for the last century— with a quarter of that century yet to come when the track originally is recorded—but later can be heard from the vantage point of an America driven to its knees in Lower Manhattan, history rendered private mythology. Picking up on the epiphanic and sanctified alto in the first song, the sax in the second is cracked and heretical, played to the end of notes in the way a writer runs out of italics, music finally reduced to words of code: *Share bride failing star*, because as pictures pin the maps of our lives, music marks the calendar.

With his sister sleeping in

the passenger seat, Parker drives the black highway spooked. He admits it to himself as much as he doesn't want to. He never has been the sort to concede fear, more adamant in that refusal than even most boys or men—so admitting it to himself now is a leap of wisdom.

Up until he was a teenager, he could charge through almost any fear except that of being alone, when sometimes at home he would wake his mother or father after they fell asleep to come downstairs with him to the kitchen, where he didn't want to go by himself.

badlands (reprise)

It's ten o'clock, although now Parker is trying to remember if he or Zema changed the clock in the car whenever it was that they crossed time zones. So maybe it's eleven, with no place in sight to spend the night. Before him unrolls the highway, if it is one. Strange lights come up behind him in his rearview mirror that he can't identify until they pass; he's driving seventy and cars are nearly running him off the road. But he feels sure that no sooner will he pick up speed than he'll get pulled over, a white boy in his early twenties in dangerous Disunion terrain, with a fifteen-year-old black girl no one believes is his sister.

He doesn't like police, and on the relatively rare occasion that he crosses paths with them, he has come to realize—with a stumble into that old mischief maker called greater maturity—that he talks himself into trouble. He almost got into it with the cop at the border a few hours back, before downshifting into deference, when the officer stared at him long and hard before waving him into West Texas. Parker's father was the same when he was younger, with no respect for any authority that was arbitrary, naively figuring that if he was in the right, he was untouchable. "You need to get over that notion," he later informed his son.

Their mother—having migrated from the new California dust bowl back to her hometown in the Midwest with the great-grand-descendants of the original Dust Bowl that brought people to California in the first place nearly a century before—tried to discourage the drive. She pleaded with her children to fly "or at least take the train." But until the manifested Towers in the Badlands took over, the news carried ongoing reportage of railway skirmishes with the National Guard, called out to seize back from secessionists control of the Southwest Chief. East of Albuquerque, the brother and sister spied a flaming boxcar, adrift like a viking pyre in the desert dawn.

Other than that it's forsaken choked Texas, Parker has no idea where they are now—that's what unsettles him. He can't see anything around him, lights of houses and buildings nearly as rare as rain, which means that nothing lies beyond the windshield but the dark. When he turns on the radio, the closest thing resembling a signal sings in static. Parker's cell doesn't know where he is either. He figures he missed a turn somewhere after Albuquerque, continuing east when he meant to swerve north, but he doesn't see any point to stopping and certainly sees none to going back, a direction he never has had the temperament for anyway.

He's glad that Zema is there in the passenger seat next to him, but he'll kill anyone who tells her. He's also glad she's been asleep since the border, though he can see at this moment she's pitched and thrashed by bad dreams. Having received no texts in the past thirty-six hours from his girlfriend, he feels especially alone and can't imagine what good even a map will do them now. Across the Texas border, however, with his sister asleep, he pulls the car over anyway to try and find—rummaging among papers on the floor and in the trunk—the map they spread out between them in their room back at the Bar Code Motel.

At Zema's feet lies their father's Log of Playlists, and in the quiet and dark of the car by the side of the road, Parker shakes the leaves of the book. Out falls not a map but, crinkled and yellowed with age, the stapled pages of an old legal petition; scouring it in the light of his phone, he reads, "STATE OF CALIFORNIA FAMILY CODE DIVISION 12 PART 4, Appeal for the Emancipation of a Minor." His accelerating fury at his sister—*trying to dump the family, the little ingrate!*—screeches to a halt only when he recognizes the misspelled scrawl that fills in the form's boxes.

only-children (right speaker)

Have these papers been among his father's playlists all this time? "Means of self-support," inquires the form, to which Parker had written, *parttime standup comic, potenchul job @ Coffe Bean*, and it all comes back to him how, as a steely-eyed, fourteen-year-old Great Self-Emancipator, he paced his bedroom plotting his break for daylight. Slipping the petition among various other school forms that required a parental signature, he got his father— self-absorbed but also reflexively trusting his son—to blithely sign everything; ultimately, of course, other legal stipulations prevented Parker's flight. In the section marked "Reasons for Petition," Parker makes out now in his younger hand, *Ever sense my sister came its ben all fucked up.*

Each always has had the psyche of an only child, with a bond that only-children forge among themselves, although Parker and Zema's bond is as singular as can be between only-children who actually are siblings. Like their mother, each always has been a take-charge person in his or her own fashion. Each was characterized in childhood by precocities, his of the imagination, hers of the spirit. Each has had recesses, hers noisier, his more sullen. Each has had furies: when he was the teen that she is now; and she still channeling or exhuming what remains of hers from childhood.

only-children (left speaker)

From the backseat of the car, the four-year-old Parker held forth on flying hamburgers that eat trees and on clouds that are igloos in the sky. The four-year-old Zema displayed insights into human behavior that her parents stopped repeating to others because no one believed she could say, let alone intuit, them. By way of natural social confidence and movie-star looks, the brother mastered anything that didn't involve numbers or school ("If I had an hour to live," he scrawled to one teacher on a paper, "I would spend it in your class, because it feels like a lifetime"), instantly drawing something original or sorting his way through a song's chords at a keyboard in an absentminded half hour. The commanding presence of any crowd, she worked out differences among contending parties in the schoolyard, achieving consensus with an empathy honed in her first two years at an African orphanage. Somewhere between gender and heritage, a black girl in a white family, Zema felt herself in crisis until an old black sax teacher, part of an expatriated jazz cohort back in the canyon where they lived, growled at her one Saturday morning during a lesson, "Confusion is the future. Embrace the confusion." While no more perfect than anyone, and siblings less by genetics or blood than law, the brother and sister also are related by one quality they share that distinguishes them from contemporaries, and that is they're true to those they would never toss aside at the first rumor or neighborhood gossip, of which both have been victim for years.

Parker's mood (take one)

Mapless, Parker figures he might as well keep driving until civilization or daybreak, whichever comes first. Privately he's betting on the sun. He resigns himself to a news station coming through better than anything else, not because he wants to hear the news but because voices out of the night are company. Their father always was listening to news when he wasn't listening to music, but Parker realizes that all the news talks about is the Towers, and the whole Towers thing has become another fear he's trying to intimidate out of his way. The reality of the Towers was slow to dawn on Parker. He barely paid attention when Zema first told him, barely gave them any thought. He figured it was some hoax or stunt, like one of those TV shows where people do crazy shit to get themselves attention, or just for the sake of doing it. Something some Vegas promoter built somewhere other than Vegas, and if it's in bad taste, well, all the more proof it was cooked up in Vegas.

Obviously there's no way they can be the actual Towers. What he remembers from when he was three isn't the event itself, which his parents, like most parents of three-year-olds, went to whatever lengths they could to protect him from knowing too much about, with the footage of planes and people falling from the sky so horrific that no parent, let alone a kid, could wrap his or her mind around it. Or maybe in fact nobody *but* a kid can imagine people falling from the sky. Maybe for no one but a kid is such a thing so naturally the stuff of nightmares. What Parker remembers is less the actuality of the event than the ever-present sense of parents no longer reliable, the first traumatic lesson any kid learns—that there are limits to parental protection. In the seat next to him, Zema is having a nightmare right now: Does she dream of someone falling from the sky? Did she find among the playlist log, and see and read, her brother's old petition for emancipation and what he wrote? "I don't want to listen to this shit," Parker declares, turning off the radio, not having meant to say it out loud. "Dad!" Zema cries, waking herself.

She turns in the seat onto her side as if to curl up and go back to sleep. But then she sits up and stares out the passenger's window. "You were having a nightmare," says her brother.

She says, "Where are we?"

"Texas."

"Where in Texas?" She leans into the dashboard to peer out the windshield, shaking herself awake.

"Across the border."

"I was awake when we crossed the border. That was a long time ago."

"Not that long. You were asleep," he adds, "dreaming."

She says, "It was still light when we crossed the border. You and that border cop . . . I thought you were going to get us thrown in jail."

"What would they have thrown us in jail for? We haven't done anything."

She blurts, "You don't have weed in this car, do you?"

"I stopped doing that," he answers, "a while ago."

"You did?"

"I smoked it when I was depressed, and it just made me more depressed."

"So," concludes Zema a moment later, "you don't know where we are," the night outside her window only proving it.

"I didn't say that," answers Parker.

She turns on the radio. "Then where are we?"

"There's nothing but talk"—he nods at the radio—"and I don't want to listen to it."

"No music?"

"No."

"Where are we that there's no music on the radio?" He watches her turn on their father's playlist. *Blood's thicker than the mud, it's a family affair.*

For a while they listen, not saying anything. Parker thinks of when their father played songs on the tiny radio station back in the canyon where they lived, and where any reputation he might ever have had as a novelist was overshadowed by his taste in music and latent talents as a bartender. People always joked (maybe) that he should give up writing books for mixing drinks, to which his father muttered, "Yeah, no one's ever said, I don't understand your martini." Now, in the car, Zema says, "Remember when Dad played songs on the radio station?"

"I was just thinking about that."

"They finally kicked him off," recalls Zema. "Why did they kick him off?"

A landmark: two consecutive unsolicited sentences about their father. "Remember we were gone awhile?" Parker says.

That was the low point for the family. They lost the house, and their mom went missing a week in Ethiopia when she tried to locate Zema's biological mother. "Why did Mom go back to Ethiopia that time?" says Zema. *Were you guys going to give me back?* she's always wondered, even as she doesn't actually believe that.

As though he has read her thoughts, Parker quietly answers, "Mom just wanted you to know. Who your birth mom is. She figured you would want to."

Zema still stares through the windshield at the road they can't see. "So they kicked Dad off the radio because he had been gone awhile?"

"I guess. Also he kept saying things between songs that pissed everyone off, like, 'Welcome to Grateful Dead-free radio, where you can listen with the complete assurance of knowing there's no possibility whatsoever you'll be subjected to Grateful Dead music.'" Then his father would play songs with titles like "Search and Destroy" and "One Nation Under a Groove." Parker says, "The more every hippie in the canyon hated it, the more he kept doing it."

"What's grateful-dead music?" says Zema.

A small animal runs in front of the car, too fast for them to be sure what they saw and faster than Parker can swerve for. "Shit," whispers Parker. "Do you think I hit it?"

"I didn't feel anything," she says. "I think we would have felt it."

"Remember that time—"

"Dad ran over the rabbit?"

"How bad he felt?" Parker can still see the look on his father's face at the thump of the car when the rabbit suddenly darted out of nowhere. He even shut off the music afterward.

Parker says, "Finally," turning up a song on the playlist, "something from my lifetime."

Catch me at the border, I got visas in my name. A Sri Lankan–Brit woman singing to the percussion of cash registers and the sampling of a quarter-century-old punk band—one of the rare instances of musical consensus between father and son. Parker was ten when this song was a hit, around the time Zema first became part of the family. "Dad always mixed up the songs," she says.

"Right?" says Parker.

"On his radio show, too. You think you're listening to one thing," says Zema, "then you're listening to another."

Parker says, "He did it on purpose."

"Did what on purpose?" says Zema.

"Mixed up the songs."

"Of course he did it on purpose," she answers, "how could he not do it on purpose?"

"Listen to this," Parker says, ignoring his sister's provocation for once and waving at the speakers in the car as the song changes. "Some Arab shit one minute, then old-school film noir themes, crazy-ass French electronica. If a song was called 'The End,' he'd put it at the beginning."

"No way," Zema protests. "That might make sense to someone. He'd put it in the middle."

Parker says, "Right?"

"And not *exactly* in the middle," says Zema.

"Of course not, that would actually be . . . *geometric.*"

"I hate geometry."

"You think I didn't fucking hate geometry in school?"

"Just don't mention geometry."

"If Dad had a playlist of . . . twenty-seven songs, he'd put a song called 'The End' . . . eleventh."

"Yeah."

"You know, because eleven is . . . the first prime number in alphabetical order. Or something."

Zema asks, "Is that geometry?"

"I could never tell," says Parker, "if he was just trying to be weird, or was weird naturally."

"*Naturally*, naturally," she assures him. "Do you think his books were weird too? Or were they the normal part of him . . . that got . . . crushed?"

Parker turns to her, more shocked than she's seen him. "Crushed?"

"Watch the road," she murmurs. *Waltzing in the wonder of why we're here.* "Some old movie guy," Parker nods at the song playing, "Dad liked those old movies, too." He says a little sadly, "Drove me nuts." *Woke up this morning, Lucille was not in sight. Maybe love is a tomb where you dance at night. In our rags of light all dressed to kill.* Georgia-bootlegger sons on the radio, industrial Midwest dadaists and Montreal poets. "But then"—Parker jumps aloud from one thought to another midstream—"when you first came over from Ethiopia, he started again. For a while anyway. Late at night, after the rest of the family was asleep."

"Started again?" asks Zema.

"Writing," says Parker. "In secret." Soho boho symbolists and Bakersfield death-row confessors and eccentrics singing Mojave blues. Detroit soulsters and Hollywood Boulevard saloon singers and old New Orleans jazz trumpeters. "This man invented twentieth-century music," they can hear their father's pronouncement, to which the teenage son would answer, "That's great, Dad. We're in the twenty-first century now."

Zema settles back in her seat. Like her brother, she accepts that there's nothing to do but plunge ahead in the black, hoping soon for a sliver of people-light or the glint of the sun. "If it was secret," she says, "how did you know?"

"Know what?"

"The secret thing he was writing secretly."

"It was not"—Parker considers his words—"a *well-kept* secret."

"So what happened with this secret book?"

"He never fin—" Parker stops. "I don't know."

"That's not what you started to say," she points out. "Did you ever read it?" and he pauses so long before answering "No" that it's almost not a pause but the end of something. Zema can't be certain if it's a confession or a lie. *I remember how the darkness doubled. Creep the ether feather, Sue Egypt. 'Scuse me while I disappear.*

final crossfade (Muleshoe)

The town they hit at daybreak is so small they pass through it, from one end to the other, in less than two minutes. Under a darkening gray sky at what might be, for all he knows, the last gas station in another night's worth of desert, Parker pulls over to fill the tank. Zema gets out to use the bathroom. *I know everyone wants rain,* Parker worriedly examines the sky as he pumps the gas, *but maybe not yet. Maybe let us first get out of wherever this is.* Slipping a twenty-dollar bill under the plexiglas at the pay booth, he asks, "Where is this place?"

Ruptured territory or no, he's learned that no one has any compunction about taking U.S. dollars, preferring them to whatever passes for Disunion currency. Behind the glass is a filament of a man only a few years older than Parker, almost six and a half feet tall and fifteen inches at his broadest point; the frames of his glasses are too big for his head, which nearly brushes the ceiling. "Muleshoe," the man in the booth answers. His height makes him appear trapped. With his red hair, he looks like a match that's been lit.

Parker says incredulously, "Muleshoe?" Realizing this sounds obnoxious, he adds, "Bound to rain sometime."

"What makes you think so?" says the man in the booth, narrowing his eyes at Parker, who chews his lip. Behind the man, who is so thin that Parker can see most of the back wall, are a couple of old indistinguishable photos, a calendar five years old, a diploma in astrophysics from the California Institute of Technology. Tacked up over the diploma is an old album cover of five guys in cowboy hats standing on a flat plain. Small white script at the bottom of the album reads *More a legend than a band*.

Nodding at the cover on the wall, Parker asks idly for no real reason, "Yours?"

"No," says the man in the booth.

"I don't mean does it belong to you, I mean did you make—"

"Doesn't belong to me and it's fifty years old so I don't think I could have made it."

"Diploma yours?"

"Yes."

"Muleshoe, huh?"

"Left California with everyone else," the other man explains.

Parker nods. "That's where we're coming from. . . ."

"Now everyone has left here too," says the other man.

"Where did they go?"

"Some moved on to other Disunion territory, for all the good it will do them. Smart ones have returned to the States."

"I heard on the news there's fighting. . . ."

"Nah, Feds don't come in unless they need to. They figure sooner or later the Rupture will devour itself like a snaaa . . ." He trails off, transfixed.

Nervous, Parker says, "How's that?" The man in the booth looks beyond Parker, who follows the line of sight to his Camry and Zema, returning from the restroom. "Oh that's my sister," Parker says too quickly, "believe it or . . ." but the man in the booth continues to stare at the Camry, its door open and music playing.

A black pickup truck pulls into the gas station. Its driver, as long and thin as the clerk behind the plexiglas but older, gets out of the pickup and also gawks at the Camry. Parker hasn't yet gotten the change from his twenty but doesn't wait, turning as casually as he can manage back to their car, conveying whatever authority he can muster.

The driver of the pickup continues staring. "Don't suppose," Parker asks to get his attention, "you can tell *my sister and me* how far we are from Amarillo?" and the pickup driver turns to him a moment, turns back to the Camry, turns back to Parker. "Sixty miles up the road is Plainview," he finally answers, "catch Highway 27 north another sixty . . . say . . ."

Slightly disconcerted, Parker says, "Highway 27?" because it so happens that the small highway running through their canyon back home is also 27. A woman gets out of the pickup's passenger side and slowly ambles up to the Camry like she's afraid she'll scare a wild, sleeping animal. *When justice is gone, there's always force*, sings the car. Not taking her eyes from the Camry, the woman digs a cell out of her jeans' front pocket and makes a call. Zema looks at Parker, who looks back at her.

Yet another pickup pulls in, apparently not to get gas but so its Hispanic driver can also approach the Camry, mouth agape. *Suddenly*, thinks Parker, *there's a lot of fucking people in Muleshoe.* Parker and his sister watch the small crowd gather around their car. "So," Parker says slowly, turning back to the pickup driver, "sixty miles to Plainview . . ." and now the Camry answers, *When force is gone, there's always* while the six-and-a-half-foot astrophysicist emerges from behind the plexiglas. It's only when the woman from the pickup opens the Camry's door on Zema's side and slides into the passenger seat that Parker realizes it's not his sister or the car they're looking at, it's the music they're listening to.

By the time the brother and sister reach Amarillo two hours later, all the other music but theirs has disappeared from every broadcasting station and radio, from every house and car. All the other music has vanished from the airwaves, vaporized mid-transmission like mist burned away by the sun. Music has gone missing from files and discs and vinyl, from cells and MP3 players and whatever CD players anyone still plays. It's missing from the confines of every interior, from the expanse of every exterior—all the music but Parker and Zema's silver Camry hybrid singing, *Here come the planes*. Behind them, the brother and sister drag the spreading silence as though it's caught on their back bumper. Thirty-six hours later, by the time they have taken U.S. 83 the length of the Texas northwest and crossed the narrow Oklahoma panhandle into Liberal, Kansas, everyone in the Midwest knows the Camry transports all that remains of American song. On the news, Parker and Zema are the only thing competing with the Towers, tracked with the intense national fascination once reserved for fleeing football stars who kill their wives.

ghost dance (one)

Once long ago, the Badlands were underwater where Wounded Knee Creek and the White and Missouri Rivers converge, now a postaquatic wasteland streaked in shades of night sky and firelight. A century and a quarter ago, the Sioux Nation spilled across fifty thousand square miles of Midwest plains that European descendants were determined to take. As the Sioux's armies resolved in the shadow of Sitting Bull's martyrdom to resist, a paiute jesus—called Wovoka by the tribes and Jack Wilson by whites—brought to the Badlands the Ghost Dance.

With the nineteenth century drawing to a close, the dance's millennial sacrament of movement and music—by which the living and dead, survivor and fallen, awake and dreamer, met at a latitude and longitude beyond topography in a ceremony based entirely on notions of love, peace, and nonviolence, with the conviction that these values would triumph over the ill will of the white government's approaching soldiers and thereby save the Sioux tribes—electrified Native and European-Americans alike.

ghost dance (two)

White people in their white cities two thousand miles away panicked at word of the Ghost Dance. The American government took the dance seriously enough to hasten the government's own agenda of the Indians' assimilation or, failing that, extermination. But Wovoka's prophecy, born of a revelation that he had when the moon passed between the Earth and sun, couldn't or didn't save his people, and few biographies since are able to tell where he went or what he did for the next forty years, other than that he lived and died under the name that white people gave him.

By the end of the first week following the skyscrapers' appearance, as the rest of the world watches aerial news footage of what is variously called Badlands Nation or the Tribes of the Towers, questions arise. To what end is the mass vigil? Is everyone simply paying tribute, and then at what point do they disperse? Does anyone believe that they're there to somehow protect the buildings, as if they could, from some horror like the one that brought them down, and if so, then for how long? Particularly following the recent, still unexplained incident involving a local sheriff who's gone missing, what is it that anyone expects to happen? For what is everyone waiting? For something or somebody to emerge?

ghost dance (three)

Some speculate that the Towers' manifestation is a second vision of Wovoka, although there's no conclusion as to what such a vision might mean. Others suggest that the Towers are the Ghost Dance's monumental grave markers. Which ghosts are being summoned is unclear: the spirits of the Towers? or the phantoms of the Badlands? Or do, within the buildings, the spirits of two decades previous meet the phantoms of more than a century past, and do they embrace in spectral communion, swap tales of their lives, commiserate and comfort each other over their deaths, display for each other photos and engravings of wives and husbands and children, some wrapped in animal skins and blankets and others donning Mets caps and *The Blueprint* sweatshirts?

Among the entire assemblage outside, who are certain—up until the buildings go suddenly soundless like the rest of the country—that music has been coming from the Towers since the first sighting, many now claim that they hear Native American chants and Sioux hymns mixing with *get ur freak on* and *thirty notes in the mailbox will tell you that I'm comin' home*. Then sometime early in the second week, particularly as it becomes evident that no one else is going to venture inside the Towers again, a mass realization overtakes the vast humanity that now numbers what is by official estimates nearly a million.

What they're waiting for is the Towers to disappear

and then for some, including those at the site watching the buildings and those watching on television and the Internet, it's into
thin air that the Towers do indeed disappear. Driving his route
yet again, the first person on record to have seen the Towers
stops his red truck with the gold racing stripes yet again where
he stopped that first afternoon, this time to gaze at the empty sky
where the buildings have vanished like they vanished from the
sky one September morning twenty years before.

But when he calls Cilla Ann and she turns on her TV to the news
stations that have been broadcasting round the clock nothing but
video of the Towers, they remain on-screen. "Maybe what you're
seeing isn't live," Aaron suggests—but why would the stations not
be broadcasting live? "Says 'live' on the TV," Cilla Ann answers,
and Aaron notices that, unlike when the Towers appeared, little
other traffic stops on the highway. Few others seem to react to the
Towers' disappearance because, he realizes, many still see them.

Soon others report the Towers missing, including more and more onlookers at the site, who wake from their campgrounds to find the skyscrapers gone even as neighbors see them plainly. It's not illusion or psychosis. It's not a matter of some not seeing Towers that are there, or others seeing Towers that aren't. The Towers are present in some photos and missing in others. They vanish from the radar of some circling aircraft and remain on the radar of others. Until it disappears entirely, the music doesn't correspond with the vanishings. Sometimes the buildings aren't there but the music persists. Sometimes the buildings are there but in silence.

More than the buildings coming and going, it's the randomness that people find disconcerting. Attempts are made to study the patterns of the buildings and music among individuals first, then larger groups. Attempts are made to break down sightings and hearings and vanishings and silencings demographically among genetic and ethnic and socioeconomic and national and conti-nental constituencies, to feed computer systems with correspond-ing data that will divine (if that's the word) patterns among the to-ing and fro-ing of skyscrapers and soundtracks. It's a century that disputes and hates the dearth of patterns, that disavows and loathes a vacuum of digitalogic, as though Someone is putting on a cosmic demonstration of the limits of the rational.

Some deduce ideological lessons, others religious designs. Some wait for science to draw conclusions that are nonexistent outside science. A theory takes hold among some that the Towers always occupy their space and that in fact it's the time around them that slips: that the Towers are located at temporal coordinates rather than spatial ones, which sometimes coincide and sometimes don't with the different traveling coordinates of each individual human being. As though the Towers always are at a fixed midnight that strikes at different times of each individual clock.

In other words, it's not the buildings that are coming and going, it's everyone watching them. In other words, the buildings have been standing at the edge of the Dakota Badlands since 7:59 and 8:28 Mountain Time on the morning of September 11, 2001. The music that everyone has heard and that now no one hears is time's audiotape, the tunes of chronometry.

Hurled from the South Tower rooftop across the threshold of his own image, Jesse has leapt from out of the future into his life. Or has leapt into the life he might have lived, another version of his life in which he's the shadow of no other man or event but rather casts his own.

Even as he has no actual sense of having lived it, he has a distinct memory of it, a life he occupied in his brother's place, in a country and century that only has known Jesse. He stops to look around at Forty-Seventh Street before heading down Second Avenue, somehow knowing just where he's going, somehow knowing every way and turn.

Candy says (New York City 1966)

At Sixteenth Street, Jesse cuts west toward Union Square, from where—when he gazes at the southwestern sky—no Towers can yet be seen, their construction still somewhere sub-horizon. On his thirty-block walk, now and then a passerby turns to look, as though Jesse might nearly be someone whom others would turn to look at, just notorious enough to have achieved a fitful conspicuity. Now and then, as though he were just one more crazy person wandering the New York City streets, he stops to shut his eyes tight, expecting the city noise around him to fade from sound . . .

. . . expecting to open his eyes and find himself back on the Tower rooftop, beneath the black flesh of a galaxy so close he can run a fingertip along the curve of the night as if down a woman's bare back. He knows, however, he really is here now, because he recalls it from before. There in the square, peering at the sky, he hears, "Jesse, darling," whispered in his ear by someone whom he remembers more instantly than he remembered his own name. But after all, Candy calls everyone darling, including herself.

NEW ALBUM REVIEWS

---

*Nothing in a journalistic endeavor (such as this magazine)
conveys more faintheartedness than a preemptive rational-
ization (such as this editorial note) preceding a piece (such
as the one that follows) unless it's the decision to refrain
from publishing at all, about which there's been much roil-
ing discussion in our offices. Originally running fifteen
thousand words that we cut by nearly three-fourths, this
"review" was submitted over the transom, unburdened
by professional representation and certainly unsolicited
by us. Reputedly a male model straight from the Tennessee backwoods, a gorgeous (or so our female staffers insist)
Davy Crockett by way of Mr. Warhol's Factory, of which
he has been a visible denizen over recent years, the author
has never published before, and nothing about him in-
stills confidence as to his credentials, by which we mean
simple command of the English language let alone grasp
of the musical concerns that were the basis for launching
this journal. Notwithstanding faint recollection of a brief*

European mini-phenomenon that surrounded the review's ostensible subject years ago and is the source of the author's enthusiasm or delirium or ire, or contempt or frenzy or wrath, or whatever the fuck it is he's saying so feverishly, fear not that any of us has forgotten Ornette or Miles or Trane or Dizzy or the lysergic-bop of the moment. So why are we publishing this, then? Because after arguing ourselves into exhaustion from one watering hole to another up and down Macdougal, we can't bring ourselves not to. All right, look: Spare us the letters, okay? We promise never to do it again.

THE EDITORS

You Ain't No Dancer (You May Be a Lover)
J. Paul Ramone & the Beatlebubs
(Vee-Jay)

Fuck Charlie Parker. Got yer attention now? 'Cause I have come, sir, to lay waste to your taste and wreak me some audio armageddon. I didn't dislodge Candy Darlin's maw from my pecker (my dead twin may have gotten the voice but I got me the words & *all* the manhood, I promise you that, ladies) and descend from my rightful throne as the most beautiful man this here Western civilization has yet produced, I didn't take on this guise of fool & boondox vulgarian—right up till I start slippin' in big words worth the $2.93 that'll buy you a long-player these days, discussin' cultural phylogenesis & all them poststructural hermeneutics that the academinx amongst you adore—no, I ain't gone to all that trouble (you looking for trouble? You come to the right place) just so now you can pay me no mind. 'Cause what I'm telling here is your story, America, no use blaming it on me. You're the one who lived it, and you fucked it up, didn't you? Sure you did.

over the whole last fifteen years, let's just say back at some juncture down at the seven hundred block of Union Avenue where the yella rooster crowed to rays of a sun rising at forty-five revolutions per minute, music might have gone a whole different direction. You had yourself colored folk near fatigued at getting shat on for four centuries and you had some pretty little white girls thinking they might like dancing with some of them fine black boys, and at that moment all anyone needed was just the right song, an anthem if you will, the sound of a black soul trapped in the right white body. But course that didn't hap-pen so what you got was the short-lived rock & rhythm craze maybe some of you jazzbos rec-ollect, a musical ghetto of queer ministers & wayward hair-dressers & blind clerks & even a few crazy-ass white evangel-icals in revolt, till that ghetto got itself put down by social inertia, moral consternation, a collapse of any strategy for resistance against the estab-lished order, and most of all a vacuum as might have been occupied by a single sorcerer who could alchemize a genera-tion's mass bewilderment into inexorable hysteria. See, I told ya I'd get to some of them $2.93 words, tho maybe those I just used go for more like $1.27.

these records that made their way overseas to ports most Americans never heard of—Calais & Le Havre & Dover & Liverpool—and I noted the whole phenomenon myself when the army shipped me out to Friedberg from Fort Hood and I lit out for, uh, well, maybe we shouldn't go into that here. Anyway, playing this colored American music were these here Silver Beatles, a Brit quintet in exile that I checked out in a scuzzy German town on the Elbe where even a man as beautiful as I who's on the run can lay his harried self low with addicts & hookers & general nefarious folk. Since the Silvers couldn't get arrested back home in England with their 'lectrified skiffle, they're performing in Germany, the larger point being (see, you surmise that amidst my digressions

I forget the larger point but I do not, sir) the band is getting better all the time and after a while have themselves something of a following. They swap out one or two weak links (no more "Silver") and then they're a quartet with a couple hit records and a real local fan base—for a while you could almost call it a *mania.*

But you know there's no getting around that part of being great is being lucky. After about eighteen months, luck runs out for our lovable moptops 'cause like every other limey sensation they go nowhere back in these Unanimous States, their records dying as fast as a hard-on when that beautiful Hamburg fräulein turns out not to be a fräulein at all, and that's all I'm saying about that particular subject. Anyway there's no call for the Silverbeebs' tunes here where the whole rock thing might have took off if anyone had laid the groundwork for it, especially with the white girls who're looking for some—well, I know no other way of saying it—funkified blackness, not pasty-ass hail-Britannia shit, and maybe I don't have to tell you that when something great is at your fingertips but the grasp fails you, well, the human spirit dies a bit, yes it does. Knowing that your chance at once-in-a-lifetime greatness is gone, you get yourself gone too or you get weird, and for a while the leaders of the band, who went by the noms de guerre Doctor Winston O'Boogie & James Paul Ramone, got weird, and then Doctor O'Boogie got gone back to Germany like the band's first bassist, who up and died from some freak headache, I'm not makin' this up, by all accounts it were a real tragedy. So then James Paul back in England got even weirder, bein' the avant-gardist of the crew to start with, developin' stockhausean loops and the whole school of chamber-cathode spatialization crossed with adolescent psychodrama.

All right, motherfuckers. Have I

played your rube long enough? Have I dropped enough g's, inverted enough prepositions? If I lend to the hayseed performance one final fart, scratch my hillbilly balls one more itch, hiccup one last cloud of rib sauce and collard greens, can we move on? Because we're getting to the best part of the story now, oh, the very best part, all you little darlings with your g's on the end, and I have come to bring you the Unholy Squall, the Black Yawp. By all accounts our Jay-Paw was a cheerful sort before thwarted providence and audience indifference gave his ever-developing musical vision its bitter edge, when he changed the band's name to its present satanic variation and returned to Germany—soon after the new album herewith under discussion was recorded—where rumor has it our hero got himself knifed by a ladyman outside the Kaiserkeller Club, his final words overheard as "there's a shadow hanging over me" or "I'm not half the man I used to be," depending who's telling it. Maybe what he saw in those last seconds of mortal-uncoiling was me, the God of Music Death, which would make this album a fitting epitaph even if its hellacious black clatter did not.

the matter of the platter, the revolver in question, a cacophonous document from music's Other Side, a hurled gauntlet to jazz's intellectual oligarchy (got to be up to at least $2.08 by now), one long-player comprising two compositions accompanied by that forsaken clankety contraption called the "electric" guitar, which once had its vogue and, hard as it may be to fathom, is known to have been played louder than Wes Montgomery. Side one is the harrowing "Barcelona (Garden of Shadows)," which may have occasioned a reunion with Doctor O'Boogie and accounted for whatever happened to Sir Paul back in Grand Teutonia, thusly raising darkly implications, what with the doctor having been ousted from his own band. With its melody fading to all manner of piano pounding, random drumming, dog whistling, gin gargling, trash rustling, Indian whooping, tubercular hacking and fellatio gasping, this first side is the sound of our crazy century dying to the rustle of its own flesh falling from our times like leaves from trees. This is followed, my brethren of the maternally betrayed and befouled, by our meisterwerk's coup de mort, much to my Memphis 'mazement, the epic that deliberates for twenty-six minutes a supposition as age-old as Eve & Adam: "Why" (little darlin') "don't we do it in the road?" since no one will be watching, until the seventh verse when, after singing the same line thirty times, our hero reveals the dawn of human treachery even before Cain set Abel straight for good (a fully excusable act on big brother's part if you know the circumstances of the thing, since Cain was God's Hit Man dispatched to kill Abel because otherwise He would have had to do it Himself), and Paulie shifts the lyric all so slightly to *"someone* will be watching," and we all know who that Someone is, don't we? the Original Voyeur. If you think He averted His eyes for a second, then you don't know gods *or* men, no you don't. God watched, yes He did, committing the Original Perversion, as the first man and woman committed the original sin, and that is the filth from which we're spawned, not the human fucking but the Deified Watching, and from fuckacide, then fratricide is the only recourse . . . anyway, we're digressing. You gotta stop getting me off track. By the ninth verse Paul is singing, "Mama will be watching," and by the tenth it's the money shot, *"My brother* will be watching," and we're back to Cain and Abel except this killing is a blow to the heart the way Mama's love for little bro was a blow to Cain, so who can blame him? Hoping the Satchmo-addled amongst ye can dig it, there's not much else to add to our evaluation of this noizelicious disc except that it puts me of a mind to relate one postscript to the whole saga, I'm sure not much more than another seven or eight thousand words [*Oh my god.— The Editors*] about what happened when I was stationed in Friedberg, where I wasn't seeing the point of all the marching & training, given that Europe still was one big shitpile from those doings in the forties, a heap of nothing but rolls & rocks and bones & bodies, not to mention all the ragging I'm taking from the sergeant and all the strange looks from the other guys, given that I am the universe's most beautiful man and I can't help that, I didn't ask for it.

take off and spend a couple of months holed up with a little fräulein who's having her prussian way with me, ripe little animal with juices flowing and well-placed enormities and, uh, wait . . . what? Well I believe I near got myself *mighty* sidetracked there, nothing you want to know about all that, I'm sure. Suffice it to say I decide to move on undercover of some night, find a boat that will sail me back home. So I firefoot it north, which winds me up in Hamburg where I hear the Silvers at one of those venues, the Kaiserkeller or Indra or Star-Club, in their early novelty anglo-blues period. Then one afternoon, lounging in one of the bars, I take note of a blonde at a nearby table dressed in black, not one of the working girls of the neighborhood, hair cut short and camera on the table next to her, and only when my eyes drift over to the gents with her do I realize they're two of the Silvers, including the one who later will suddenly drop dead like I mentioned before and who now, this afternoon in the Hamburg café, goes off with the blonde, leaving alone at the table Doctor O'Boogie, and I suddenly become aware that as I've been watching the blonde, he's been watching me.

look that makes me uneasy, cursed as I am with the beauty of the spheres. But that's not the way the good doctor is conjecturing me. His mouth is smiling but his eyes are *thunderin'*. He's got a beef with me, and since we never have met as far as I can recollect, I can't imagine what it might be, but it seems we're going to have words and the only question is who's going to meet this tête-à-tête head-on. So I scoop up my beer and saunter over and say, "How ya doing?"

"Yeah," he says, which doesn't exactly sound like an answer to what I asked, "have a seat, mate," indicating one of the now unoccupied stools at the table, "why not?" and the way he says it is a bit hostile to tell the truth, and I'm wondering what's his querulous quandary. I sit down anyway, decide

I'll *enchant* the son of a bitch. "Been seein' you around the clubs," I say, "gettin' a big kick outta what you and your pals are up to there."

"Is that right?" he says. "Well then I guess it's all sorted, innit," and everything he says is sarcastic like that, "because *you* get a big kick out of it," and I'm a bit steamed but keeping up the enchantment offensive as best I can.

"Maybe make yourselves some records," I suggest, "bet you could do all right."

"Oh you think so, do you?" he says. "Think we could cut some records, could we?"

Yeah, I just said that, asshole. But "why sure I do," all Mr. Southern Charm.

"Well we're on our way then, there's nothing to worry about, is there?"

Uh, "Okay."

"Because *you* think we could do all right if we make a record, yeah."

"Look here, pal"—I had me enough—"I don't know what exotic brand of national-socialist insect got up your anus but I'm just trying to be friendly-like, figurin' I wouldn't mind talking to somebody for once who can say something I understand, and seeing as how I caught some of your act. What did I ever do to you anyway?"

And he leans across the table as far as he can, so as to get his face as close to mine as he can, as if just asking me to take a pop at him, and looks me in the eye and says, "You were fookin' *born*, mate. That's what."

the way it's going to be with the good doctor. "Well, sir," I say, "not much I could have done about that, no."

"That's debatable," he says.

"Not really," I shake my head, even laughing a bit, can't help it, and all this time he's got that smile that doesn't go with anything else about him. "Let me ask you," he says, "can you sing *anything*?"

"Why of course I can sing," I say, "any Southern boy can sing himself up a storm. I'm a *fine* singer."

"Right, well then"—he leans back on his stool, finally pulling his face out of mine and folding his arms across his chest—"let's hear something."

"How's that?"

"Sing, *It's one for the money, two for the show.*"

I clear my throat, give my tonsils a bit of a warm-up—"Mi mi mi mi mi"—clear my throat again. *"It's one for the money!"* I let go with it. *"Two for the show!"* Everyone in the bar turns to look and for a second he just sits watching, smile never changing, eyes never changing, arms still folded, and I figure he and everyone else are just trying to comprehend how the mellifluosity of my tone can match the splendor of my visage. "Oh brilliant, that was," he finally says.

"I told you," I agree triumphantly, and only then realize that he doesn't think my singing was fine at all! He leans back over the table again and hisses, "That's a sodding disgrace," practically spitting in my eye. "We gave up *him* for that?"

"Uh," I say, telling myself

I'm confused but maybe not so much, "'him' who? And who's 'we'?"

"We is the bleedin' human race, that's who."

I'm telling myself I don't know what he's talking about but I have a feeling in me as if, all of a sudden, my heart is a stone sinking not to my feet but something deeper. "What do you mean, 'him'?" Saying it, my voice breaks, I barely can get it out.

Who knows? Maybe he hears the shudder in my words and it doesn't make him exactly pleasant but he relaxes a bit, pulls out a smoke and lights up. Studies me and then says, "Forget it," waving away the whole thing.

But I guess he knows I can't forget it. "What do you mean, 'him'?" I croak again.

He takes a drag and I figure he's going to blow it in my face but he doesn't. "Part of being great," he finally says, "is being lucky, innit? You're in the right place at the right time, they"—he nods his head out the bar door—"are ready for you. They been waiting all along for you. Billy O'Shakespeare comes along a century earlier, same bloke, all the same talent, and what's it get him? The Black Death or smack in the middle of the War of the bleedin' Roses, some King Henry and some King Richard at each other's throats, yeah. Or he's born in the middle of the Chinese countryside—fookin' lot of sense anybody's going to make of *Hamlet*. Instead fate plants him upstream from London, most elvis town in the world, Liz the First on the throne, Johannes bloody Krautberg's printing press invented in time to run off all Bill's plays so everyone can read 'em." He says, "It's a bit of conspiracy then, between the bloke who's doing the telling or showing or singing, and that lot doing the listening or watching or dancing. And if one side or other isn't in on the conspiracy, what good is it? Let's be coconspirators then, that's what you're asking them, and you better bloody hope they're, you know, *in the fookin' mood*. So here's how it is," he says, putting out his smoke and leaning back over the table. "Paul and George and Pete and even bloody Stu, if he still fancies it, we'll make our records just as you say, we'll have ourselves a time, for a time. Maybe have a bit of tiny glory for a few months back home. But then it'll be over, and the way it *might* have gone, that way where we might have changed the bloody world, that way where nothing would have been the same after us . . . isn't going to happen. Because that's by way of America, no getting around it, much as we'd like to. Doesn't matter how much those of us over here resent it, it's all about America if, like I did, you come out of the fookin' sticks to take over the world— and there's nothing in sodding America for us now, is there? Because you Yanks will never have a clue what to make of us, because *he* was the beginning. I mean, Lonnie Donegan is all well and good, right, but *he* was the Big Bang, and *he* never happened, *he* never gave anyone a glimpse of what it all might have been—and I'm not talking about the music, am I, since we're all just stealing the music from the spades in the first place. What we're talking about is the Moment, that's what *he* was, we're talking about how before him there was nothing, and we got bloody you instead, didn't we, you who can't sing a lick. So I'll do this awhile and then go back to me pencils or brushes or teach art to the future me's of the world, just like all me fookin' teachers who never could do anything else and tried to teach me." He gets down off his stool. "*Three to get ready*—that's the next line of the song. But no one will get to number three because we needed *him* to get us there, and *you*, mate, there's no bleedin' point to you at all."

Well there, Mr. Editor, maybe

we just want to cut [*Editor's note: In this section of the original manuscript, the ink of the type is stained and the words smeared—perhaps, we can only speculate, from the tears of a sobbing author—in such a way as to be unreadable*] this whole last part because [*more streaked type*] I surely don't know what [*unreadable*] get into all this anyway, except I suppose it seems some enlightening part of the saga, like I said before, one of your dark preludes. I think maybe I'm done here. But you haven't yet read the final testament of the God of Music Death. You haven't yet heard the final crashing note of my calamitous Day of Reckoning. I've just begun. Because when there's no point to a man who's liberated of any dictate or purpose, when a man is not just born out of his own time and place but is one for whom there's no time or place at all—that is a man truly unconfined, sir, *a man on the loose.* I will make my own point till there's no song to be heard anymore by anyone. Till the world is deaf of the most distant descant and every last bird is throttled of its chirp, and the chiming of every passing breeze is asphyxiated, and no musical land exists free of what I map. I will make my own point, till not the land but the map itself is the point.

J. G. PRESLEY

tracks 03 and 04:

"Wooly Bully" and "Tomorrow Never Knows"

One spring in the mid-1960s [writes Zema and Parker's father in his log], twenty years after the twentieth century's defining conflict, in which good and evil will be so incontestably delineated for the final time, the cover of an American newsmagazine poses in stark red letters against a black background the question IS GOD DEAD? having no way of knowing that time is a shadow-highway of successive roundabouts with After occasionally preceding Before, and that two responses five thousand miles apart already have been recorded within days of each other and within hours of the magazine hitting the newsstands. The first answer, a bilingual countdown (*Uno! Dos! One two tres cuatro!*) to American chaos by way of Texas (via Memphis), is: Who cares? The second, an atonal cosmic yowl recorded in a London studio— based in part on the Tibetan Book of the Dead and in part on the convulsions of the singer's ego—with hybrid western/ eastern percussion and a musique concrète sound design of loops and fragmented human voices, is: What does it matter? A leading cultural commentator of the time identifies the four musicians of the second song as "imaginary Americans," America representing the source and fulfillment of their dreams and an idea big and rapacious enough to claim the musicians as Americans, in the same way that America claims anything it chooses to, including the demise of the divine.

Originally a B-side from Veracruz by way of Pacoima, sung
in Spanish, the first song is a fifties hit, a cover of a recording
from half a century earlier when records barely existed. The
Mexican-American singer is seventeen, lost and presumed
dead a year later when, on tour in the Midwest, he "wins"
the coin toss that puts him in the seat of a doomed single-
engine Beechcraft Bonanza; he is mourned by a Latino L.A.
that needs a survivor more than a martyr. In fact, dazed and
confused, on February 2, 1959, the young troubadour lifts his
head from the Iowa snow to ponder the small plane's smoking
rubble, then painfully struggles to his feet to walk . . . where, he
doesn't know, and later can't say exactly how long it is before he
comes to find himself in the land of his ancestors. For the next
twenty-five years, as all other promises he makes to himself
fade with youth, he holds on to the one to his Mexican family
of a better life in the land of his birth. Many nights he risks
everything attempting to cross an unforgiving border, from
the other side of which—once he's finally made it to safety—he
will send for his wife and children. "It's only a matter of time,"
he assures them. The evening of his final try, well into middle
age and slowing down, he holds his wife close and whispers
in her ear, as he always does, that everything will be all right.
But this time he has a funny feeling, and she does too.

When she was eight, in

the backseat of her father's car driving through the canyon where they lived, Zema would see in the center village the brown men gathered beneath the trees who had hitched rides from the coast six miles away. They waited for someone like Zema's father to come hire them to trim trees or build a fence or repair a driveway or paint a garage door.

If Zema's father parked in the village to mail a letter at the post office or buy his daughter corn chips at the general store, the brown migrant workers would stand from where they sat beneath the trees and wonder if he had work for them. "Nothing, sorry," her father would say.

stop even if he needed to, because he hated telling the brown men he had no work for them. Sitting in the backseat, Zema became afraid when she heard people talk on the radio of how the men she saw through her window were criminals and smugglers and drug traffickers. The news spoke of the men as a horde, advancing across a border barely a hundred miles away.

Characterizations of the brown men were especially vivid to the eight-year-old of a different brown, evoking as they did animal stampedes and locust clouds. Before her father turned off the radio in disgust, Zema would be startled by descriptions of the insect-people as physiologically misshapen from massive quantities of narcotics that they hauled in secret. She worried that when her father told the migrant workers, "Sorry, nothing," they might become angry, although they appeared only disappointed, if they appeared any way at all.

One afternoon, the

younger brother of one of Zema's classmates tumbled twenty feet down a crevice behind a neighbor's backyard. Crushing part of his small skull, the four-year-old oozed life onto the rocks while medics and the fire department above surveyed the ravine helplessly for where the boy might be located under the growth and brush. The event electrified the canyon within minutes. It brought to a standstill the traffic that poured from the northern valley to the sea along another Highway 27 that shared its number with the small road that Zema and her brother would drive out of Texas years later. A helicopter fluttered indecisively with no idea where to set down in order to haul the boy up. Crowds gathered and Zema held her father's hand for the final time that she ever would, as the two watched with everyone else the first responders who called the boy's name. Then, as though a moon passed before the sun, the hillsides went dark from the migrant workers descending onto the overgrowth of the ravine. With machetes, they hacked away the brush until, within minutes, the four-year-old was revealed. Hoisting above them ladders from the fire engines, the migrants formed a bridge across which firemen clambered, harnessing the boy, who was lifted by helicopter and transferred to the nearest hospital. Undergoing brain surgery and emerging from a coma, he walked out five weeks later with a steel plate in his head—a lid on his life, in which Zema imagined that now and then she might see the flash of the canyon sun.

As Parker and Zema cross from Kansas into Nebraska, with the gray clouds above that look like rain—except these days the clouds always look like rain, especially the clouds that never rain, which is all of them—scorched desiccation bears them into the future. Having hijacked all music, Parker and Zema penetrate deeper the continental center as more flags display the traditional thirteen red and white stripes with a black field where stars ordinarily would be. Some feature an incensed and glaring Jesus, sandy hair pushed back behind his ears like a biker's. Others depict a former president X'd out in red, the way newsmagazine covers used to X out deposed tyrants and wartime enemies.

As much as possible, Parker sticks to the highway, where the Camry can't be intercepted. As best he can, he times his approach at traffic lights so as not to come to a full halt. But at an otherwise empty four-way stop in a suburb outside Dodge City, in seconds the neighborhood emerges from their houses, a hundred people pouring out of doors across their lawns. Surrounding the car, shaking it from side to side, the people pound the Camry roof and beat at the windows. A chant rises: Let us hear! Let us hear!

People jabber at the car in tongues, runic utterances of vague and undefined horrors that Parker and Zema don't understand: *katyperry! coldplay!* "What's the matter with all of you?" Parker cries. With their Camry stalled, he starts rolling down the window to reason with them, but Zema pleads from the passenger seat, "Don't roll down the window!" locking her door. To the glass beside her, people press their faces or ears. "We're not a jukebox!" Parker tries to tell them. "It's just our dad's old playlist!"

A woman in her seventies sticks her head in the car through Parker's rolled-down window. "What's that?" she says to the song she hears from the car. *Here come the planes, so you better . . .* Turning to her white-haired husband in outrage, she feels violated that this should be the first music she's heard in days. "Why would anyone listen to a song like this?" the wife demands of her husband, who pays her no attention but looks at Parker and opens his mouth wide to let something slither out, *gratefuldead* uncoiling hideously from his lips.

It isn't clear to Parker and Zema whether the flags along the road running through Texas, Oklahoma, Kansas, and Nebraska fly over territory officially ruptured, "official" being a misnomer since none of the declarations of Disunion are recognized by anyone other than those who make them. This underscores that no one comprehends what's happening other than that no one believes in the same country anymore and probably never has. Crossing state lines, Parker has heard of people presenting passports and in some cases compelled to sign Disunion pledges considered in other states felonious and potentially treasonable.

That the president X'd out on the flags hasn't been president for five years doesn't devalue his currency as a figure who rallies those who hate him. To the Rupture he embodies Year Zero, his successor counting as no more or less relevant than Year One or maybe Year One Point Five. There's no dismissing the public-relations value of the former president's color, the same as Parker's African sister; that Zema makes no mention of the flags doesn't mean she doesn't note them. On the highway she sinks down in her seat and Parker stays out of the fast lane, where he fears the silver Camry is most conspicuous.

By North Platte they're fugitives of a kind, though they've broken no law and no highway patrol is in pursuit. No APB is out on them. To the contrary, their music crosses boundaries with impunity; entering the Rupture, where Parker expects time and again to be stopped, the car is waved on by border guards. Soon Parker realizes, *They know it's us and have been told to let us through.*

When Parker's girlfriend was institutionalized in Vancouver and then prohibited from contact with the outside world, her texts ended. Undeterred, Parker shared his membership to a music-streaming site with her, communicating by telltale song titles. "When will I be loved?" he asked. "Reach out, I'll be there," she assured him. "Where did our love go?" he called from a melody in flight, growing distant. "Somewhere," was all she had time to speculate, "over the rainbow."

Now, with all the songs gone, this means of contact vanishes as well. Their relationship fades into either a narrow escape or a forever-lost moment of happiness—Parker won't know which for years. Nomads for whom west has swallowed up all other quadrants, with growing futility he and his sister try to stay one town ahead of urban legend and word of mouth. Filling once–Top Forty airtime with reports of Parker and Zema's progress, DJs announce excitedly, "Kids, Supersonik is on the move!" The siblings' trajectory becomes anticipated: "We project they'll hit the state line by tomorrow eve! So keep us posted on *all* your latest sightings."

Behind them grows a caravan. Other cars pull alongside in the next lane, drivers and passengers leaning out, motioning for Parker and Zema to roll down their windows. Helicopters follow. Slipping pursuit and stopping to sleep, the brother and sister park the increasingly notorious Camry in the darkest corners of motel lots. For meals they slide the car into the darkest alley; at various eateries along U.S. 83, Zema waits in the car as Parker gets takeout. When radio isn't obsessed with the brother and sister, or a sheriff who went into the South Tower not to be seen again, it reports that the Towers disappear in thin air and reappear: two big silver Post-its from God, thinks Parker, that She's not fucking around anymore.

Aerial dusting where the Towers were/are is undertaken to determine if they still stand. In video shot by those who no longer see the buildings, dust rains down, covering the ground, while video shot by those who still see them reveals dusty buildings. Some suggest that maybe one of the planes no longer showing structures on its radar should fly through the space to determine the true extent of their absence, but most find the idea of flying a plane into the Twin Towers—even into space where Towers might no longer be—offensive and intolerable on any level, psychological or symbolic.

In the meantime the music that America sings flees. It flees American lips and American ears, particularly that America which claims to be most American by desecrating everything America is supposed to be. When Parker and Zema drive past Rupture flags, when they roll by the barbed wire of Disunion, there rise from the ground swarms of aural detritivores, a monstrous termite sound that feasts on music-death and leaves a pall. Deafened earth rolls before the siblings, one horizon of sedition and perfidy following another, strafed by those who most proclaim America's embrace.

Speedometer set to the haste of moonlight, fifty miles of silence later Parker and Zema turn off the sound system, only to still hear music. They stare at the powered-off receiver, the music faint as though from another car or passing house. Parker turns the receiver back on, back off. "I don't get it," he says, glancing around the interior of the car for an answer, across his shoulder into the backseat. "Just watch the road," says his sister. When she has fallen asleep he can almost swear he hears an old nineteenth-century folk song his father used to like, except with different lyrics: *Oh shadowbahn, I long to ride you. Roll away.*

Parker says to his sister, "Don't you hear it?" Growing louder ten miles south of the Dakotas, the song announces their afternoon arrival as the Camry rolls into the outskirts of Valentine, Nebraska. With a field on one side of the street and an Assembly of God church on the other, a pack of forty boys not a lot younger than Parker immediately engulfs the car. Crowds are becoming less friendly, Parker and Zema have concluded silently and independently of each other. With a baseball bat, one of the bigger boys taps the window on the driver's side.

The brother and sister look at each other. The boy outside the car with the bat taps on the window again, more forcefully. Finally Parker rolls it down. "Hey," he says.

"Get out," says the boy.

"You're stealing our car?"

"Don't, Parker," murmurs Zema.

"They're stealing our fucking car." Parker turns to her, then back to the boy outside his window. "Don't hurt my sister. You hurt my sister, I'll run you motherfuckers over," he says, pointing at the people in front of him.

The boys' leader peers in. "Your sister? If you say so. We don't care nothin' about her. Get out."

"What are we supposed to do without our car?" says Parker. In the distance, overturned satellite dishes skitter like toadstools across the plain. "It's them," the boy outside confirms to the others gathered, waving the bat.

Parker looks back at Zema. "Are we getting out?" she whispers.

"I guess we either give them the car," her brother answers, "or they start smashing it up with us in it." He opens his door, and Zema opens hers.

The cell phone with their father's songs sits in the cradle beneath the car radio. "Don't forget that," Parker says to his sister, nodding at the cell, but Zema leaves it. "You hear me?" he says.

"Leave it," she whispers, and grabs Parker by the wrist when he reaches for it. She looks at him more pointedly than he can ever remember. Over Parker's shoulder, the boy with the bat says, "That what's playin' your tunes?" indicating the cell. "Yeah, you leave that the hell alone."

"The fuck," Parker says, leaving it.

Brother and sister back away from the car. Parker stands in the street with arms folded, glaring at the crowd of boys, as Zema turns and heads in the direction of the church.

Music fades from the car and then is gone.

The crowd stares stupefied at the now silent car. The boy with the bat looks at Parker. "What did you do?"

"We got out of the car like you told us to," says Parker.

"You turn it off?"

"I didn't turn anything off."

Laying his bat in the passenger seat next to him, the boy sits in the driver's seat. He searches the dashboard. "You turn off the car?" he asks again.

"The car's still running," answers Parker, "it's a hybrid."

One of the other boys puts his hand on the car. "Still runnin', Ray," he says to the one behind the wheel. "One of them city cars that don't make noise."

In the driver's seat, Ray says, "How come we don't hear nothin'?"

"Like I said," Parker tells him, "it's a hyb—"

"The *tunes*, not the fucking car! Why don't we hear the tunes?" Ray picks up Zema's cell. "Is this on?"

"Oh my God," Parker mutters under his breath.

Ray jumps from the driver's seat with his baseball bat. "What did you do?" he says, starting toward Parker ominously.

Parker can see Zema in the far distance by the church. "You said get out of the car," he replies, "we got out."

Ray cries, "You turned it off!"

Parker spreads his arms and opens his hands. "I haven't turned off anything."

"Then where'd they go, dude?" Ray asks.

"They . . . ?"

"The tunes!"

The other boy who had his hand on the car's hood looks at Parker. "Music was playing when you got here," he says. "Are you guys really Supersonik?"

Ray is adamant. "They are."

"Why not now? The music," says the other boy.

"Don't know," Parker answers.

"Bullshit!" Ray explodes. "This is highly frustrating!"

"I *feel*," Parker offers as calmly and reassuringly as he can manage, but the other boys circle him and close in. "You know what?" he tries to explain. "We're just going to Michigan to see our mom."

"Hey, Ray?" says the other boy, and for a moment the sheriff standing twenty feet away is confused, thinking the boy has called her name.

The boys turn to look at the woman in her midfifties with the gray hair tied back in a short ponytail. A moment of quiet later she says evenly, "Everyone go home now."

Ray gazes around at the others, smiling. "Who are you?" he asks the woman. He sees the badge on the sheriff's lapel and says, "Is that real?" and she answers, "No more or less than this," pulling the coat back to reveal the occupied holster around her waist. She's been driving from the Badlands since fleeing the South Tower, when she ran out onto the buttes in the dark; with the multitude waiting, she turned and fled past the other Tower to the north.

She headed for the other side of the bend that Aaron rounded in his truck before the Towers appeared, and hasn't stopped since. Hasn't had the radio on, so doesn't know about Parker or Zema or Supersonik; all she hears is the whistled song in her head that accompanied a beckoning memory. Far enough from the Tower, she figured the song would fade, but the song hasn't faded. She can't outdrive the whistle, heading south as though she has no idea where she's going. But she does know where she's going, really—the only place there is for her to go; and she knows that she knows.

jurisdiction (two)

Pulling into Valentine, spotting the young black girl in the distance at the top of the church steps, the sheriff is not only out of
her jurisdiction, out of her state—she's out of her country. She's
out of her life. She's not worrying about jurisdictions anymore.
She is her own jurisdiction, the same way Jesse has become his
own map. She tells Ray now, "Everybody wants to know what's
real. Everybody asks is this real or that. Are they real or not."

Ray says, "What do you mean, 'they'?"

"You know what I mean."

Ray finally sputters, "Aw, just go away, old woman." But she hears
his voice break and knows she has him, that he knows what's real
enough. Eyes level with the other Ray's, voice as steady as the other's has grown shaky, she says, "I'm going to tell all of you one . . .
more . . . time."

The boys surrounding the car slowly disperse. Flashing at the
sheriff what is futilely meant to be a defiant look, Ray gives the
side of the Camry a last kick, leaving a small dent before he wanders off. Parker starts to yell something at him but stops himself.

Regarding the sheriff, he thinks, *I take back half of everything I've said about cops.* He walks toward his sister waiting on the church steps, calling to her, "Let's go." Watching what's left of the crowd, Zema calls back, "Who's that?" meaning the woman in the distance.

"Let's just get out of here."

Checking out the church over her shoulder, Zema answers, "I'm going in. You go find some food, come back in twenty minutes."

Parker says in disbelief, "You're going to church?"

"Come back," Zema says, "when everyone's gone."

A few remaining boys watch Parker pull away in the Camry. In silence he drives till he finds a Frosty's, where he gets burgers: *I'm sick of burgers*, he thinks. *If we were back in New Mexico, I could get a taco.* Zema is waiting on the church steps when he returns; checking the empty street, she moves quickly to the car. "Drive," she says in the passenger's seat.

"Food." Her brother indicates the takeout bag on the floor.

"Drive."

"I counted four churches between . . ." and trails off, listening.

The music is back. Parker hits the gas as the volume rises, hurtling them down the first road taking them out of earshot.

Radio Ethiopia

When Zema first came to the canyon as a small girl, the family called her Radio Ethiopia. At first no one noticed the music, and then everyone thought what they heard came from somewhere else, or that it was only the girl constantly trilling to herself. At dinner Zema would be admonished for singing at the table. Finally her mother realized it was the girl's body humming, that Zema was a transmitter picking up, sometimes miles away, their father's radio broadcasts. It made Parker crazy. "Make her stop!" the ten-year-old insisted.

Over time, Zema's music did stop. Whatever frequency she broadcast from the beginning of time, knocked off by family drama and personal trauma, occasionally returned in an uncommon moment of terrestrial reconciliation as mysterious to the girl as to anyone else. Now back out on the open road in the middle of the night, in the last desolate miles before the last state line before the Badlands, Parker has finished his burger when he says, "It's you, isn't it?"

Pointing at the cell, he says, "The songs are transmitting through you," then pointing at her, "at least until you get too far away. Just like," he snorts, "the good old days." They ponder this in the dark awhile. "What happens if we turn off the cell phone?" he says.

She answers, "I think you need to turn *me* off."

Nodding at the field beyond the windshield, he says, "Maybe we just get rid of it, open the window and toss it."

For a while she doesn't answer and then, quietly, "Can't do that. All Dad's songs."

"Be nice if we could at least turn you *down*." Several miles of silence pass before he blurts, "It wasn't your fault," and although she looks at him as though she has no idea what he's talking about, and although the subject never has come up between them, or come up between Zema and anyone, she knows exactly what he's talking about. She says, "Something you've had in your head all this time and just been waiting for the chance?" He can feel her staring at him but keeps his eyes on the small splash of road in the headlights preceding them.

She turns in her seat again, her back to him, her inner life always having been even more locked away than her brother's, even if she never matched the stoniness of his silences.

"I've messed everything up since I came," he barely hears her whisper now. For a moment he can't figure out why the words ring such a bell, until he remembers the emancipation petition he found however many nights ago since Texas, and that he now knows for certain she read. Her whisper is full of not simply despondency and torment but grief, the grief of someone in mourning her whole life, grieving for that life's lost source, for the lost family that she never knew and the found family to which she never believed she belonged. For the lost code of identity and the secret message of the self that she never deciphered or disclosed.

An unfamiliar wave of sorrow for his sister overwhelms him. "Zema," Parker says, "I was younger than you when I wrote that petition," although he doesn't suppose that this can be of solace to her; he doesn't imagine she feels that young. After enough silence passes that he isn't altogether sure she's still awake, he says, "Zema?"

"Dad signed it," he hears her answer.

"I know," he says, "that you feel like you understand everything when you're the age you are now—"

"I don't feel like I understand *anything*. . . ."

"Well then you're smarter than I was. Because it never was about you, and the truth is that, even then, I sort of knew that. But there you were, and you happened to come along when everything around the family seemed to come apart, and you made yourself easy for everyone to blame since," he says, trying to make a joke of it, "you *are* a pain in the ass." If she laughs, he doesn't hear it. He sighs. "Are you listening?" She doesn't respond. "Zema?"

"I'm listening," she says, her back still turned to him in the seat.

In the middle of a nowhere so black that around them the fields vanish, they drive on. Suddenly more seized than ever by the importance of being older, he explains, voice struggling, "You know all those forms they make you bring home from high school? Permission for this and requirements for that, waivers and disclosures and shit? So I slipped the emancipation thing in with the others and took them to Dad, and he glances at the one on top and signs everything—oldest kid's-trick in the book, right? And you *know* that sounds just like Dad. So be mad at me if you want," says Parker, "but not him. At least not for anything other than being clueless half the time. Which we both know he was."

Only as the volume of his sister's music falls off, becoming barely audible, can he be sure she's asleep, her channels changing violently as she dreams of their father. Having entirely lost track of their direction, Parker can only assume that they're still heading north, since they're still heading the same direction that they were heading a while ago when that direction was north. For long enough to lose track of time as well as their direction, he thinks of his girlfriend and tries not to cry, struggling for control in that way that his father always recognized when the boy was more upset than anyone else knew. Adrift in these thoughts long enough to no longer be certain who's calling him, finally he concentrates on a distant voice: *Wake up*, it says; and finally he recognizes it as his own—and far away Zema transmits a song too low for him to make out. *Wake up* . . .

. . . and with a start he wakes. He's terrified to realize, for a moment that now feels like hours, that he fell asleep at the wheel. It can't have been longer than a couple of seconds, just enough to start veering off the road; if you want to wake yourself up good for the rest of a drive, try falling asleep at the wheel for a moment.

But he wakes to his heart pounding, and to a new, open interstate much bigger than what they were on just seconds ago. Pulses of dull light flash alongside them, and other than the dim illumination of the pulses, the highway appears to be entirely unmarked. In the one or two seconds during which

Parker fell asleep, the low distant song that his sister broadcasts has opened before them like a tunnel, with the pulses of dull light to each side passing faster and faster until they're single streaked blurs: and then, with growing excitement and further

adrenalized by his own hammering heart, he hears himself silently exclaiming, *Is this it? Have we found it? the secret highway!* and over and over he whispers, *Zema!* or believes anyway that he's whispered his sister's name only to realize he hasn't, that he's uttered to her nothing but a shadowhisper, and that there's no point at all to any consultation since they pass nowhere any diversion or exit as they continue to drive, if what they're doing can be called driving, this one-way thoroughfare with only its single escape at either end of it—assuming they haven't just disappeared into thin

three

earshot

The first song is released to little notice on September 11, 2000. The second is released in March 2003, the same month that—in the name of the incendiary millennial moment that follows the first song by exactly one year—the country invades another that had nothing to do with the moment. *All the words are going to bleed from me*, sings the second song, which becomes the year's biggest, recorded by a Detroit ex–husband-wife team posing as brother and sister who could be twins. The song's opening guitar riff turns into a stadium chant sung together, in unison and full-throatedly. Soldiers drive their tanks across Middle Eastern borders humming the riff, pushing themselves onward to the song's insistent opening seven notes. Opposing armies hum the same notes back, bolstering their spirits or fleeing with it in their ears. "Pilots" also is written and recorded by a male/female duo, from London rather than Detroit: *Armored cars sail the sky, they're pink at dawn* forecasts that morning exactly one year later. Does its ethereal melody float above the clouds with Atta and al-Shehhi in the cockpits of American 11 and United 175, airliners pink in the sun before rendered the red of fire and blood? On opposite sides of a chasm, are these two songs infused with the spirit of a stillborn nation that wanders its own landscape trying to make sense of destiny, trying to make sense of survival, trying to make sense of which twin country is really left? Which is the corporeal and which is the ectoplasm? Which is the reflected and which the reflection? Which is the sun and which is the shadow?

when midnight comes around

and Jesse wakes, he really has no idea what time it is in the vast emporium where it's always midnight, regardless of whether, outside, it's two in the afternoon or two in the morning. Whatever dream he was dreaming already fades. Was he in the Tower again, back on the roof of the world where nothing is in the distant dark but moonscape and the twinkling of a thousand lights, back atop the world's highest building that he seems to dream of every night? if he must concede it's a dream, which he has nearly convinced himself it must be, since he can't remember how or when he actually would have been in such a high space, the winds such as to blow him from where he stood into another place and time.

Yet it all has the vividness and emotional specificity of not a dream but a memory. The song that made its way into his sleep still plays; he can't be sure, wondering to himself, if it's a recording or Andy's new little kraut blonde singing from the next chamber. "Must be evening," he decides out loud, based on the doings around him, and then sits himself up in the corner of the cavernous room. A series of Moroccan arches link every foiled silver wall of jagged mirror shards to the adjoining red wall. Junkies shoot up in whatever dark corners where couples of indistinct gender aren't fucking. There's Gerard with his whips, Mare gyrating before a projection on the wall of Andy's latest: naked people—mostly guys, so Jesse surely doesn't need to see *that*—down at the Mad Hatter Diner not doing anything much, like in all Andy's movies. Janet from upstate, lately calling herself Viva, railing in her fashion about Catholics. Paul, scowling little Nazi mick on the prowl with his fucking camera like he's C. B. goddamn DeMille. Jesse catches sight of a woman on the other side of the room glowering at him, all ferocity.

Val, well shit, Val, li'l dyke psycho, disheveled jeans and work shirt, folksinger's cap pulled down on her crazy little fucked-up head, bedraggled and agitated and barely able to stand in her own footsteps: glamour-killer if there ever was. *Hell*, thinks Jesse, *she be unhinged by even the standards of* this *place*. She just keeps scowling at him and then it comes back—was it earlier this afternoon he ran into her outside, stalking the steps and lying in wait so she could hit somebody up for some bread or give Andy her latest treatise on lopping off all the men's dicks, assuming she can't suck one in the meantime for fifty bucks?

Jesse told Val to skedaddle and thought he ran her off but there she is now, who let her in? Couldn't have been Paul, always threatening to beat her up—well hell, even Jesse would never lay a violent hand on a lady, stretchin' the definition of the word mightily to include Valerie. Just a few feet away from her, where he's been every night for the last two weeks, is a silver-haired gent in a wheelchair saying nothing, just watching, small smile. Assume it's a he; in this place you never can be sure. Jesse still is unsettled by the blow job Candy gave him last week. No way Candy can be a he, Jesse assures himself, dismissing from his mind the gossip and overheard chatter.

But then there are people who aren't so sure about Jesse, for that matter, which is just *stupid*. Jesse thinks about this awhile crumpled in the room's yawning corner that's one of the only sources of light, besides, 'course, Andy's latest movie projected on the wall. Also projected is the now celebrated double image of Jesse in cowboy shirt and holster but no hat, six-gun drawn, looking like the superstar that he is, just on the basis of everyone saying so. There in the corner, with the piercing glare of the projector in his eyes, Jesse covers his face.

Crawling out of the light, Jesse scurries *like pestilence, sir* (self-revulsion), to a darker corner. He realizes he's hungover. In the drone of yowling thorazine cello, he gazes into the dark of the room, eyes adjusting to the Sunday clowns and femmes fatale with their streetlight fancies, whiplash children in ermine furs and blackened shrouds and shiny boots of leather . . . but realizes maybe the hubbub is losing its charm. Not the same since Edie left, Jesse mulls with a small pang in his heart.

Maybe, he thinks, this move down to Union Square will recharge something. Why hell, back on East Forty-Seventh you got yourself wandering folk who are downright mentally disturbed. Or maybe, he thinks, it should all just die, the whole damn scene. "What are you doing down there, cowpoke?" comes a voice from out of the dark above him that's not quite male, not quite fe—

Candy, goddamn it, do you have a dick or not? Jesse peers up at her. *Have you* ever *had a dick?* "Catching me my beauty sleep, darlin'," says Jesse.

"Is that all it takes?" she says. "Maybe I should go to sleep and never wake up."

"Speaking of dead," Jesse nods, "do it all seem a might moribund to you tonight?" No one had to worry if Edie had a dick, sweet little dollop of New England maple cream that she was.

Candy says, "It's midnight. It's early. You know the witching hour is two. Give it time, it will be fabulous. It will all be very bop, very elvis," and she looks at the projection of Jesse in the other corner. "Maybe everyone's waiting for *you* to make it happen . . . so make it happen, baby. You know I hate the quiet places that cause—"

"Say, darlin', don't mean to interrupt what I'm sure is a very poetic thought," he says, nodding across the room, "but who's the old earl over there coming in on wheels every night?"

Jesse has noticed that the man in the wheelchair with the silver hair is watching him. *Oh my good lord*, thinks Jesse, *another Factory-slumming fancyman checking me out*, except that when the man's attention does turn elsewhere it's to Mare slithering nude across the floor with cat-o'-nine-tails in hand—so maybe the aristocrat's interests don't run Jesse's direction after all, at least not in *that* manner. Rather the old man, smoking a thin cigar, regards Jesse in the way that Jesse remembers being regarded once before by a young Hamburg exi in black, like someone who knows something from beyond the present moment, as it's currently defined.

Gazing over her shoulder, Candy says, "My God, what's she doing here?"

"That's a she?" says Jesse. "Man, I don't hardly know as how I can stand the confusion."

"Not *him*," says Candy, "standing right next to him—isn't that Valerie? Didn't Andy excommunicate her, and isn't it someone's job to keep her out? Why is she looking at you like that?"

"They both giving me the eye, though I feel something close to certain not for the same reasons—can't hardly say about the old guy. . . ."

Candy shrugs. "He's not *that* old. Still this side of fifty—old but not *ancient*. Hair went all white just last year."

"What's wrong with him?" asks Jesse.

"Degenerative something. Got a beautiful wife, I hear, he never spends any time with, up in Bridgeport or Boston or New Haven somewhere. Very rich in the chord of D . . ."

"Decadent," says Jesse, "downright defiled."

"Definitely."

"Deranged, demonic . . ."

"But destined too, as I understand. He *is* giving you the eye."

Jesse says, "You know that's not my style, darlin'," but looking down at him on the floor Candy chuckles from so deep in her throat that, even in the dark, he finds it discombobulatin'. She says, "I'm pretty sure he likes the girls. The girls who are girls through and through, of course, just . . . like . . . *you* do, cowpoke." She leans over and touches Jesse's nose. He has the feeling there's a joke he's not in on. "Destined?" he says, trying to recover.

"As I hear it," she shrugs again, "he was in Congress or something. As I hear it, once upon a time, he was going to be president of the United States."

Through the rippled dark, in the swoon of the electric tempest wailing around him, Jesse makes his way across the room.

Perfectly still, the other man in the wheelchair with the white hair never takes his eyes off Jesse's approach. Jesse pulls up a small round table and chair. "Well, sir," he says, having to shout over a rise in the soundtrack, "buy you a drink there?" The other man just raises from his lap a cocktail glass before taking another puff on his thin cigar, appraising Jesse ever coolly.

Wondering that moment if the old man can speak at all, Jesse sticks out his hand, "Jesse," and the other, shaking it after a moment's hesitation, answers simply, "Hello."

"Mind if I sit?"

"You already have."

"I'm, uh"—Jesse gestures at his projection on the wall—"somethin' of a superstar around here, you might say."

The man in the wheelchair barely glances where Jesse has indicated. "Congratulations," he answers flatly, one corner of his mouth hardly turned up.

For a few moments, Jesse tries to place the accent. "Boston," he finally assesses. "Like to think I got me an ear for such things, being a cosmopolitan sort—say, bet you're a friend of Edie's." Now he can see Candy was right: Up close the man in the wheelchair isn't really that old. It seems to Jesse that he takes uncommonly long to answer the simplest thing, constantly measuring every response in the same way that he constantly measures the person across the table from him.

It's not that he's hostile, exactly. He's remote, his constant appraisal of Jesse unshaken, mouth verging on a smile that's slightly mocking even as the target of his mockery is unclear: maybe it's Jesse or maybe it's the man himself, or maybe just the situation. "Yes, well, I don't believe I've met her," he says from the wheelchair with the slightest shake of his head, slight smile never changing, eyes never leaving Jesse, "know a bit of the family, of course. They go back pre-Revolution. Long before my own."

Wildly optimistic that this is the beginning of an out-and-out conversation, Jesse nods, but when there's no more, he answers, "Okay, yes sir, pre-Revolution you say," and now the white-haired man is back to his coolly observant regard, watching through the thin smoke rising from his fingertips. "Well you would know if you had met Edie, she's fine, or was." Jesse nods at the naked woman with the cat-o'-nine-tails snaking past their feet in the dark. "That there's Mary."

The man nods. "Those days are over for me," making the slightest gesture at his chair, but Jesse isn't really sure which days he means.

Crazy Val has moved to the middle of the room, still watching. She appears more disturbed than ever. "Val there"—Jesse points—"you might want to stay clear of. She got herself this notion to wipe out all the menfolk."

"How's that?"

"All the male folk. She's even written herself a play about it, articles and the like."

"How's that supposed to work?"

"How's what supposed to work?"

"Killing all the men. I mean, after they're all gone."

"Yeah, well, you got me there. Not sure Val's got an answer for that one, or maybe she doesn't care. I hear you're in government of some sort."

"Not anymore."

"What was it you said your name was?"

"I didn't."

"No, actually," says Jesse, "I didn't think you had."

"Jack," he says, and looks at the projection of Jesse with his six-gun. "So what is it *you* do, then, uh, when you're not being . . . what did you say?" and for the first time he flashes a smile. "A superstar?" The smile becomes broader. "You're not in the movies, are you? You're not a singer by chance." He adds, "I've known some singers."

A chill overcomes Jesse. It's a handsome smile, the other man's, maybe even dazzling there in the dark, taking the edge off his mockery only slightly. Everything he says is wry, sardonic, dry as sand—but now there's something else too, something underneath. "Well, sir, I could have been a singer," Jesse protests, and Jack answers, "Is that right?"

"Yes, sir. Except I gone into the writing game—right at this here moment I have a magnum opus in the pages of *Round Midnight* magazine."

"Can't say I know it."

"Newly reputable jazz journal," Jesse explains, "of course I'm not aware if you're cottoning to jazz—don't know as how I ascertain much about the subject my own self. In any case I've become a man of letters."

"Last refuge," Jack nods, "of the socially impotent."

"Say what?"

"What's this, uh . . . magnum opus about?"

"Why . . ."

"Jazz?"

"Not exactly, it's about . . ." Jesse shrugs helplessly. "Why, it's about . . ."—he throws open his arms—". . . everything!"

Jack says, "Well of course it is. Everything that every writer writes is about everything. I doubt there's ever been a single word written by any writer who's ever lived that wasn't about everything." Jesse glares at Jack, assessing whether he can just get up and leave rudely, as is his inclination, or is bound by some social grace to be more polite than either the other man or the conversation warrants. "I used to be a writer myself," adds Jack.

"Is that right," says Jesse, just as the other man said it a moment before, in just the same tone.

"Journalist . . ."

"Did you write about everything?" Jesse seethes.

"I wrote about history. Published a book or two. Won an award or two. Then I thought, Why write about what you can change?"

"So you changed everything then."

"No," Jack says, leaning as far across the small table as the prison of his body and chair allow, the smile vanishing as quickly as it flashed, "you did."

Jack says, "What you and I share is how each of us was supposed to be someone else. You understand that, don't you." It's not a question.

"No."

"Everyone," he says, relighting his cigar, "talks about . . . lessons of history when what they really mean are"—he seems to ponder the cigar a moment—"*auditions* of history. History always auditioning for one last performance that's never delivered because it's always rewritten. To, uh, talk of the 'lessons' of history suggests . . . models that can be applied to other instances, when no moment really is enough like another that any model applies, without turning the model into something that's so much something else as to make it, well, not obsolete, but not all that relevant either."

I'm certain I don't understand a thing you're saying, Jesse thinks, staring fish-eyed at the other man, who laughs, "I'm certain you understand exactly what I'm saying." Jesse contemplates slugging the man. "So," the man says, slightly puffing his cigar, "all that, uh, Marxist theory about the *science* of history . . . you know, cause and effect, how there aren't really any Great Men . . . wants to turn history into math, or an equation, take out the variables of, well, people, when you and I both know—"

Calm down, Jesse tells himself.

"—you and I both know that if there's one lesson of history," says the man in the wheelchair, "it's that part of being great is being lucky. And that means the rest of us being lucky as well. So if we really know anything about history, we have to accept the . . . caprice—"

"The what?"

"—the random. Swallow hard the fact that if we . . . shift Churchill or Lincoln off their place on the timeline by a hundred kilometers here or a hundred miles there, or a decade here or there, then everything turns out differently."

"Well now, that's all mighty interesting," says Jesse flatly, "that's all *real fascinatin'*. So if y'all excuse—"

"That's why," Jack continues without the slightest indication that Jesse has said anything at all, "the only sort of writing that can't possibly be about *everything* is history. The whole point of the historian"—he takes another puff as cool as his regard for the other man—"is to convey an understanding of the general, when more than anyone the historian is a registrar of happenings. Taking stock of the specific. I suppose that from a narrower perspective, I have you to thank—I'm alive, after all, if you call this living," he says, looking at the steel cocoon enveloping his bottom half, "spine crumbling like confetti without a hard-on to my name. From the perspective of a dedicated hedonist in the Indian summer of his years, I suppose this *is* preferable to dead martyrdom, if we can forget, you know, the vanities of immortality. Anyway," he adds, "dead martyrs aren't here to tell us otherwise. Are they?"

Once, on the eighth-floor balcony of a hotel overlooking a square named for a World War I general, a candidate for president of the United States surveyed the city before him and all its high black windows in the surrounding buildings, where a more paranoid man might have imagined enemies lurked with long-range Italian rifles.

But such grand paranoia was premature. *I haven't earned it yet and now never will.* Just inside the suite's double doors, out of sight from anyone who might have happened to look up and spot him standing there incongruously, the candidate had set his crutches, which he never allowed the public to see him use when his back was killing him, which was almost all the time.

jigsaw

As the presidential candidate gazed out at the square and the broken summer sky above, for a few seconds on the balcony it was the quietest that it had been since he arrived in Los Angeles a few days before, fully prepared to accept his party's presidential nomination. Behind him, bedlam overtook the hotel suite so completely as to ignore the candidate, who was the subject of a furor that was some mix of dismay, panic, and wrath among all the campaign's young turks.

Out on the balcony the candidate wasn't especially startled, only slightly bemused, to note that a piece of the sky was missing. The entire azure ceiling from east to west was hairline fractured, filled with fine and nearly imperceptible cracks like a well-assembled jigsaw puzzle, except now one part had gone astray and in its place was just black. It wasn't the black of outer space but rather blankness, its absence revealing nothing behind it. From the hole in the blue, musical notes fell like rain.

The candidate's typically cool remove had taken hold. This was the white-heat calm that kicked in when anger or fear or excitement reached critical mass—the protective detachment in an overwhelming situation, from do-or-die presidential primaries to wartime Solomon Islands torpedo-boat mishaps to sleeping with the wrong damned woman. Always in a state of dying, he thought in such situations: *It's only life, which is over soon enough anyway.* Moments before, in the suite watching events spiral out of control on television, reflexively the candidate had looked around the room for his younger brother.

It was one of those instances when the two caught each other's eye and shared a secret understanding. Then he remembered his brother was on the same television screen that set off the uproar. With howls of betrayal and invective escalating among his managers and lieutenants, and with the candidate apparently the calmest man in the room but for the fact he was silently seething, on the TV his brother on the convention floor—amid the Illinois delegation in the process of falling apart—looked up at one of the cameras.

Staring straight into the candidate's eyes from the TV screen, knowing his older brother was watching from the hotel suite three miles away, the younger man had a look on his face that asked, Do you believe this? No, the candidate mouthed silently, then: Yes. Actually I do. I actually do, now that it's come. I think I knew this would happen all the time. Parting the bedlam with everyone else oblivious to him, he had hobbled on his crutches out to the hotel balcony, the sounds of the city below serene compared to the tumult behind. Twenty-four hours before, the chant of the thousands who surrounded the sports arena where the convention was taking place—*We want Stevenson!*—could be heard even from here.

Now the candidate felt that consternation roar up behind him from inside the suite when someone opened the balcony door. "It's Bobby," he heard over his shoulder, the aide holding the telephone in one hand and the receiver in the other. "Calling from the convention fl—"

"Yes," Jack said, "I saw him. Just now"—he waved toward the suite—"on television."

"He's wondering . . ." The aide trailed off.

"Tell him to come back to the hotel."

"He says—"

"Just tell him to come back. It's over."

There was a pause. "I should tell him that?" the aide choked. "That it's ov— . . . ?" and he couldn't finish, and the candidate said nothing more. *Fucking Illinois*, thought the candidate, his mind free-associating everything from the past four months, *if we just had won Wisconsin more decisively*, only to dismiss this line of thought: *Wouldn't have made a difference, Wisconsin was a blessing because it made West Virginia necessary*, which made the case for his candidacy all the more irrefutable when he won there so commandingly . . . *ninety-five percent Protestant!* except it wasn't irrefutable after all, was it? the case for that candidacy being refuted at this very moment . . .

. . . not just refuted but demolished, with all the delegations— Illinois, Iowa, Kansas, California—going to pieces, like the sky. By the time his younger brother returned, the suite had cleared out without anyone saying anything to the candidate they had failed, who still was on the balcony where he had remained nearly an hour, excruciating as it may have been for him to stand so long. Sometimes he peered over the edge at the street below—trucks from the network news, the print press, everything in commotion: *They loved me until a better story came along.* The candidate snorted. He was detached from this betrayal too, a man who understood expediencies.

"Where is everyone?" he heard his younger brother say—not so much a question as a livid accusation—in the balcony doorway over his shoulder, where the aide previously had been with the telephone in hand.

"They heard you were coming," the candidate chuckled. *I make them nervous but my black-Irish runt brother fucking terrifies them.* When there was no answer, the candidate turned back to find the doorway empty again, and then returned to the suite to find the other, smaller man slumped in a chair, surrounded by the campaign's wreckage both literal and figurative.

Phone wires and flyers, empty glasses and cigarette butts sometimes in ashtrays and sometimes on the tables and floors. The gold leaf of the ceiling now dingy, thick carpet pockmarked with stains. "Funny," the candidate said, "how something can come apart so quickly," staring at the TV that was dark for the first time in a hundred and thirty hours, a year of work gone in an afternoon . . . well, not one year but four, really—or did he mean a lifetime?

"Funny?" asked his brother hollowly from the chair.

"See that sky?" Jack gestured with his thumb at the balcony behind him. "There's a piece missing."

Bobby glared at him from the chair. Was his big brother being metaphorical now? Ironic? *Literary?* Did anything other than a spectacular pair of tits unruffle him? Pulling up another chair, the older man sat, leaned forward, put his chin in his hands. "So," he said, pondering as he would eight years later in the shadows of the Factory, "Adlai again . . ."

The younger brother nodded. "Yes."

". . . three times—?" It *was* pretty hard to believe. With gathering ferocity Bobby raged, biting off the words. "Every one of them is . . . going . . . to . . . pay," but Jack just shook his head as his brother went on. "*Every one of them*, because like . . . like . . . William Jennings Bryan," he sputtered, "Adlai isn't going to make it this time any more than the last two. Especially if the other side winds up going with Rocky . . . but even if they don't . . . and then our time shall come, *next* time, and when it does—"

The candidate kept shaking his head. "This was our time."

"—every one of . . ."

"Or, it would have been, if it weren't for, you know . . ." He nodded at the balcony.

"If it weren't for . . . ?"

". . . you know . . . like I was saying. The sky."

"Are you *singing*?" Bobby had never heard his brother sing in his life. Everyone thought Jack told Bobby everything, when the truth was that Jack didn't tell *anyone* everything. "Just something

I heard out there," Jack nodded at the balcony again, where the sky rained a song. Everyone thought they were close, the brothers, and in these electoral crucibles they were closer than they had been, and closer to each other than to anyone else; but it was a new thing, what fraternal closeness there was, born of recent years and the common appetite for power, most of all any power won competitively. "He's bound to offer you veep," said Bobby. "Whether he wants to or not—"

"No."

". . . well, I doubt he wants to. But he's bound to. Two mornings ago you were sixty votes away from the nomination, so he's—"

"No," more emphatically.

"That's what I say too."

"We tell him to go to hell," said Jack, "like he told us last winter when we offered him State for his support."

"Adlai doesn't say, 'Go to hell,' it's beneath him. He's too elegant for it. Adlai says, 'Please kindly recuse yourself to the nether regions.' Quotes Dante while he's at it."

"The party will never forgive me for it, when I say no." Jack looked his brother level in the eye. "The party will say I need to take it, for the party."

"He could have put you on the ticket four years ago. Of course that would have meant actually making a decision. Making decisions is beneath him as well."

"He doesn't want to offer it and we don't want it, and neither of us has a choice. Except I'm saying no anyway."

"Good. Next time."

"I'm telling you, there isn't a next time. It was now or never."

Bobby said, "You *are* singing."

Jack laughed. William Jennings Bryan! "I heard it outside."

"I thought we got over the Catholic thing in West Virginia."

"Coming from a hole in the sky. What is that, anyway?"

"What is what?"

"That song. *It's now or never.*"

"I like show tunes."

"I don't think I could have just made it up."

"I've never regarded you as musical."

"You know, I think I *did* just make it up. Just now. Well," he said as his little brother glared at him, "the sky made it up." Jack added, "It wasn't the Catholic thing."

"The girls?"

"What about the girls?"

"Do they know about them?" Bobby had never approved of his brother's girls.

"They?"

"Anybody. Any of them. Do any of them know about the—?"

Jack said, "Everyone knows about the girls."

Everyone knew, he admitted to himself for the first time, after always having convinced himself that no one knew. After always having convinced himself that, by implicating everyone around him, including his brother, in his deep dark secrets, those deep dark secrets became theirs to keep as well, secrets for them to keep from themselves like he pretended to keep them from everyone else. "It's not the girls," he said.

"Someone leaked the medical records," said his brother.

Jack shook his head. "It's not the girls, it's not the medical records. Lyndon already knew about the medical records. It's not the Catholic thing. I keep telling you"—he pointed at the balcony—"go look for yourself."

"I don't want to look for myself," said the younger one.

"The . . . zeitgeist is missing a piece."

"The what?" Bobby never had heard his brother use a word like this, any more than he had heard him sing. "You hate people who use words like that."

"There's no *sense* to me."

Bobby said, "I don't want to talk about this anymore."

The older brother stretched in his chair, pain now wearily crawling up his already disintegrating back. "Do you have a cigar?" he asked.

"You know I don't."

"Aren't you the keeper of my cigars?" laughed Jack. "Who's the keeper of my cigars around here? I guess I have to keep my own cigars from now on." A phone rang in the suite two rooms away. "Adlai," said Bobby to the sound.

"Or Dad."

"Dad . . ."

"Calling as usual to tell us it's all going to be great, it's all going to be fine. Just a small obstacle—"

"Ohhh," Bobby moaned into his hands.

"Adlai wouldn't be ringing here. Well"—Jack shrugged on second thought—"he might."

"Should we answer?"

"Of course not."

"But if it's Dad?"

"Especially," Jack answered quietly.

"You're still singing."

"Am I? Are you sure it's me?"

"It's you."

The now former candidate asked, "I mean, why should I be president?"

"Because," his brother answered, "you're better than them."

"Let's say for the sake of argument I am. What makes me better?"

"Smarter. Tougher."

A thought flickered across Jack's mind but he lost its train. "It's not about smarter and tougher," he said calmly, "*you're* smart and tough enough to know that. It's not even about wanting it more than anyone." He pushed his back up from out of the chair and moved slowly, more slowly than he should have wanted anyone to see him move. "Where's my coat?" he murmured to himself, and his brother didn't answer because he knew he wasn't expected to. Moving from one room of the suite to the other, Jack settled into his customary glide, the difficult mobility that he managed to persuade the outside world was grace. Fumbling through his pockets when he found the coat, he pulled out the cigar he had expected to be smoking under other circumstances.

Back in the room with his brother, Jack lit the cigar and stopped to look around the suite, for the first time taking in how empty it was. "Last one." He raised the cigar to show Bobby but was still really talking to himself, still murmuring. "Now I just need a blonde." Bobby put his face back in his hands. "It's about the moment," Jack continued, "forging itself. From all the previous moments. In the case of an election, say . . ."

My God, thought Bobby in horror, *he's waxing philosophical.*

". . . it's about everything that the country has been before . . ."

It really *was* over.

". . . coming together now to be whatever it will be . . . next. The only argument for making me president is because we've never lived in times like these and no one like me ever has been president before. But if we're not *really* in times like these—"

"What do you mean if we're not really in times like these?"

"—if the times aren't really what we thought they were"—he pointed at the darkened TV—"then Daley and Illinois just say, Fuck Kennedy and let's go with our own guy even if we already ran him around the track twice against the same Republican— albeit at the bottom of the ticket—who already beat him twice, because at least this time they won't have the General at the top so maybe it will be different. That's what they tell themselves, any- way." His younger brother stared at him blankly. "Part of being great is being lucky."

Bobby blurted, "Bullshit," and Jack laughed again. "Bullshit" was downright epithetic for his self-righteous little tough-mick choir-boy brother; he wasn't sure he ever had heard Bob say "bullshit." But then Bob never had heard Jack sing, so everything was altogether unraveling this afternoon, wasn't it? and the older one studied the younger awhile. Momentarily jettisoning his usual aversion to reflection, he thought, *This is my little brother's failing, Bobby believes life is supposed to be fair or, if not fair exactly, then serial, consequential, a sequence of things that lead to other things that are led to by the earlier things. Randomness, caprice, the errant happenstance of a shot fired (or not) from a depository window, or a song that falls (or doesn't) from the sky that changes (or doesn't) the world and all its possibilities—none of these fit in the little Jesuit's moral scheme of things.* "Why should I be president," he posed socratically with no heat or reproach, "I who am . . . nothing if not the triumph of somebody else's idea of our era, somebody else's idea of what the times are," *except we got you, didn't we, Jesse? the twin of no possibility.* Jack considered his younger brother now. *You of all people understand about brothers.* "So," Jack sighed grimly, drawing a final puff on what would have been his victory cigar and finally absorbing the enormity of what had been lost. "I suppose this means my chances of ever fucking Marilyn have gone out the window."

The songs of American bullets, the choir of American gunfire: As the slug whistles through a Dallas afternoon on its way to the presidential target, does it sing "You Go to My Head"? The music of American murder, which is not to say the music of American murderers, because the murderer himself has no music in him but rather only the melody of his weapon, which is why he loves it so. All the reports of American weapons are dulcet, the murderer loving his weapon for the music of which he himself is humanly empty, not a single refrain to be heard snaking its way from his foul soul to his foul mind to the foul tip of his foul tongue, along the foul passage of his American being.

Why is the sound of something always said to be within "ear-shot"? So, Jack sighs to Jesse eight years later from the prison of his wheelchair in the Factory shadows, "you best have a moment that's forged from the thing you might like to think that you manifest." He takes a last drink from his highball. "You best," he says, "have a moment already . . . catalyzed by an *irresistible* presence, a moment already defined in fortuitous terms—and I do not mean Frank fucking Sinatra. Otherwise there's that . . . missing piece of the sky, some crucial shard, some . . . indispensable color gone from . . ." trailing off.

He says, "You might have all the money in the world. Well, not all the money, but enough. You might have a ruthless and powerful father determined to do what it takes. You might have connections and operations and the campaign to deliver West Virginia. You might have the good luck of running against the weakest field of opponents imaginable, opponents who haven't the slightest chance of unifying enough party delegates to be nominated for anything. But that isn't lucky enough if you also have barely a Senate term and a half, if you have no record of distinction whatsoever, if you have little credible experience on the world stage, if you haven't established yourself as the most compelling spokesman of the day's most compelling issue, whatever that might be, if you haven't even an underwhelming equivalent of, say, a Cooper Union speech. Then you better be lucky enough to also have a forged moment in which your youth, and your embodiment of a new world overturning the old, commends you. Otherwise, when the time comes and everyone stares up at the convention ceiling and asks themselves, So other than the money and looks, why exactly is it again we're choosing him? they may find their attention wandering to someone with prospects no better than yours and perhaps worse, just because you never really gave them a good enough reason to do otherwise."

The thin cigar stops midway to his lips. "Instead, ignoring what . . . *fate* encoded in the genes, out you came in some tide of afterbirth that washed away your other, better, more brilliant, more magical version. Instead of getting the twin of possibilities, the half who might fire an age, we got the half who coughed up cold water all over it. Sheriff Stud with his six-gun," waving at the projection on the wall, "desperado king. Can't you at least have some of this crazy poon here"—he gestured at one of the naked women on the floor around him—"blow you while I watch, so I can begin to grasp what it was all for? Aren't you good for at least that? Because it's the closest I'll ever come to my glory days, when the pussy of the world was in flower. I'd rather have had half my presidential head blown off in—of all cars!—a Lincoln, yes, I'd rather that than *this*." He slams his fists down hard on the wheels of the chair. "I'd rather be immortal, fuck you very much. Airports named after me and a myth better than my life ever could have been no matter how hard I tried. *They*," he says, pointing at some invisible throng beyond the walls, "would rather have had that, too. They would rather have had the Other Me like they would rather have had the Other You. Nobody ever wanted *this* you," pointing at the projection, "*at all.*"

Valerie

For the last several minutes, Jesse has been nearly levitating from his seat. Now he leaps up with one hand knocking across the room the small round table that's been between them, and lands on the crippled man, flailing. By the tenth or twelfth blow, or maybe fifteenth or twentieth, Jesse's resolve to beat senseless the man in the wheelchair morphs into a new intent, to throttle him where he sits. It's hard to be sure in the din and drone of the room whether anyone's taking note. A thought exultantly flashes across Jesse's mind, *Good lord, I do believe I'm going to kill this here motherfucker,* as though he might then be free of himself, when he sees the blood on his hands around Jack's throat. "What the—?" and then he sees the trickle of blood running down Jack's chest from the hole in it. Jack sees it too. He peers down at himself, he and Jesse looking at each other in mutual confusion, Jesse uncurling his hands from Jack's throat to gaze at his red fingers. The sound of the gunshot from seconds before registers with Jack before it does with Jesse, first one man then the other turning to look at the crazy disheveled woman in the cap pulled down on her bedraggled head.

At the crack of the gunfire, the surroundings finally seem roused from preoccupation, people surfacing from drinking and dancing and fucking and shooting up to note something even more out of the ordinary than what's ordinarily out of the ordinary. Val still holds the small thirty-two-caliber Beretta, dervish of smoke writing from its barrel like that from Jack's cigar. Viewing the small bubbling red hole in his chest, Jack looks back at first Jesse, then Val, a gurgle of blood at his lips. "My heart," he agrees, "well, my least vulnerable spot. Better my heart than my h—" when Val shoots him in the head. "Damn!" Jesse cries, launching himself backward from the wheelchair and the body in it. He's sprawled across the floor staring at the dead man in disbelief when a third shot whizzes by, nearly grazing Jesse's cheek; a startled cry comes from somewhere behind. Val fires again, bullet piercing the floor a foot from Jesse's hand, and then again as he frantically rolls behind the other man's body, using it as a shield. Around him, Jesse can sense the dispersal of the other denizens, who have shrewdly concluded that his proximity isn't where they want to be. He peers over Jack's body to see the woman turn the gun on herself, not putting it in her mouth or up against her temple but rather confronting it point-blank, as if she wants to study the bullet's emergence and journey from the barrel to her brain. The hammer clicks instead on an empty chamber and then another. She flings the gun at the ground, disgusted at yet one more betrayal in a world of weapons made by men.

All the twin songs change places in the light and the dark. "Dancing in the Dark" is written in the third year of the Depression. A love song, it also can be heard as a tune of defiance (*we can face the music together*) before one national dark displaces the next, until the looming prospect of nuclear obliteration's atomizing light is so bright that everyone can only wish for a dark in which to dance. Renditions come and go, not to mention the song's title, which later is used for altogether different songs. In a Hollywood studio musical of the early fifties, the song becomes a ballet, but the most terrifying version is performed by the ballet's dancer in another context entirely, on a recording in which the singer slows down the song to the tempo of the small jazz combo accompanying him and delivers the lyric at little more than the volume of awed dread that occupies the song's heart. One hears, over the singer's shoulder, the darkness yawn to swallow him. Another two decades later, "Dancing in the Dark" is answered by "Spirit in the Dark," written and sung by a minister's daughter. *All of my brothers,* her song announces midway, *move with the spirit, all of my sisters* . . . the dark reasserting its promise of sanctuary, a reminder that light isn't always life and that the death that God brings is better than that brought by men. We know what the dark is, the black woman sings to whatever white audience listens, because you taught us. You kept us there for three hundred years, so now let us guide you to it. Dance a little closer, a little deeper in the dark.

The first song is composed in 1949, recorded by artists both black and white before its definitive rendering by a blind rhythm-and-blues revolutionary in the same year as an American president's assassination. On that same murder-day, the second song is composed by two young men born and bred in the California beach towns south of Los Angeles, the writing begun before the trigger is pulled and finished after the bullet tears off the president's head—so who's to say what epiphany explodes in the course of that bullet's trajectory? Can *the warmth of the sun, it won't ever die* only have been written before the gunshot, or only after? Is the song transformed—without any writer or singer having altered it—simply by the moment with which it coincides? Does "That Lucky Old Sun" have greater ramifications because its most comprehending interpretation turns the song from desperation to grace? Do its implications become more momentous only because that definitive performance coincides with not only the year a president is assassinated but also the year that an Atlanta preacher delivers to a quarter of a million people, before the country's greatest monument, the greatest American speech of the American century? Both songs are sung in the shadow of the sun they claim to extol but actually distrust. They're songs not of the sun's warmth or light, but rather the singers' memories of warmth once but no longer felt, light once but no longer seen.

When Jesse opens his eyes, damned if he has the slightest idea where he is. On waking, he's never sure whether he's back high in the Tower beneath the roof of the night, or how he ever would have been there. The first thing he sees is the steel outlines of twin constructions framed in the window next to him—and then he remembers he's in a holding cell at the police precinct on Vesey in Lower Manhattan. Somewhere in the building a woman bellows, "Cut them off! Kill the scum! Death to the testosterone rex!" as Jesse's eyes rest on the unfinished Towers' rising steel girders.

He wonders if they'll be gone like a Boeing 767 with his first blink. He doesn't so much recognize the Towers, since he only saw one from the other in his earlier existence, and since a hurricane can't be recognized outside the eye from where one leapt however long ago it's been. But even the Trade Center's skeleton evokes something familiar, the scaffold of a memory, a home that never was. In his cell window the nearly full moon is caught in the metal brace of what someday will rise to become the second Tower's ninety-third floor, a glowing white sea-castle in a sky-aquarium filled with the fish of swimming stars.

After establishing in cursory fashion and with stony neglect that Jesse is unscathed other than the ringing of gunfire in his ears, for hours the next morning police batter him with questions. What was his relationship with the shooter ("I don't got no relationship with that crazy woman, sir, I don't believe she has any such relationships"), what conspiracy was concocted and what were the motives ("I never before in my life met that there congressperson, can't possibly imagine why anyone would want to kill such a fine fellow"), until—precinct eyes narrowing and lips pursing—the questions begin to contradict each other.

When Jesse is returned to his cell, Val's invectives of the night before have gone silent. Someone brings him a burger and Coke. The course of the day passes; a public defender comes and goes, having no more conversation with Jesse than is necessary to identify himself. An officer informs Jesse that federal agents are being brought into the case given the victim's identity. At some point Jesse is returned to the interrogation room for further questioning, where he waits another hour before being returned to the cell with no interrogation having resumed. Almost forty-eight hours after the shooting, another officer unlocks the cell, releasing Jesse with no explanation and no charges filed.

As he departs police headquarters, the first thing that Jesse sees is his reflection in a bail bondsman's window across the street. Then out of the reflection pours the throng of reporters waiting on the sidewalks, television cameras rolling in on waves of the same questions he's been hearing from the police for the past day and two nights, at greater velocity and volume. Microphones drop before his face like tarantulas from trees.

Dazzled by flashbulbs and dumbfounded by voices, Jesse barely can say anything. "Don't know nothin'!" he keeps shouting down the block and up the next, journalists and TV vans in pursuit. The continuing chase gathers passersby, people emerging from shops and galleries angrier and more threatening, curiosity transforming into something vaguely vengeful. Jesse is to Soho before he shakes them, ducking into a bar and out its back exit, and doesn't stop running.

His first instinct is to head toward Union Square before it occurs to him that the Factory will be swarming with more reporters. *Oh, Andy must surely be lovin' this here damn tumult.* Better to chance his own tiny hotel room on West Twenty-Third, safely slipping in through the side door; at some point a *New York Post* grabs his eye, and his hand grabs it in return.

Only once in his room behind his locked door does he read, under the headline PANDYMONIUM! and the subhead FORMER W.H. CONTENDER SLAIN IN DEN OF DEPRAVITY, that "by all accounts, and according to the reported statement of the alleged assailant, the actual target of Miss Solanas's attack appears not to have been the onetime Massachusetts senator but a flamboyant male model identified as part of the Warhol harem and traveling freak show," *uh, wait a minute, wait wait wait,* Jesse thinks, mind racing.

Flamboyant male model? "They wouldna called *him* flamboyant, mate . . ." answers a voice from the past, five and a half months later, when summer gives way to autumn and the reporters are gone with the curiosity hounds. Jesse hasn't returned to the Factory since the shooting. At four o'clock on a Thursday afternoon, he's nearly alone but for a clerk in a Third and Macdougal record shop that winds and rambles and tumbles with platters in bins and on shelves. Two other stragglers wander in and out before the clerk behind the counter continues, ". . . would they?" looking straight at Jesse.

It's the voice that Jesse recognizes first, or maybe the tone more than the voice itself. Jesse has to look closely before placing the Brit, smoking a cigarette and appearing to have aged twenty years in the past eight. Sallow, wearing Benjamin Franklin eyeglasses, and carrying an extra fifty pounds, he either has lost all his hair or cut it off. "Sensational, yeah. Rockin', I imagine. Maybe even the King," he says. "But not *flamboyant*."

Sarcasm as toxic as ever, the clerk says, "Thanks for the review, by the way. Of course nothing it said had anything to do with anything, not anything true anyway, but I'm sure Paulie would have been thrilled if he were still with us, bless his bloody free-bootin' soul. I believe we even sold a copy or two here in the shop to a couple gits, restraining myself as I did from breaking it over their heads."

"What y'all doin' in these here parts?" is the only thing Jesse can manage to drawl.

"Well," Doctor Winston O'Boogie answers, "now that's one right cracking tale, innit? But not one I'm of a mind to tell, if it's all the same to you. Doesn't much matter, really—I'm as outta place here as you, and that's pretty outta place, since you're outta place anywhere and, thanks to you, so am I. We're outta place together, aren't we. But I tell you what. I been waitin' for you to cross my path again sooner or later, figuring we were bound to since we're both so outta place—I think I've just been holding on to this job long enough to give you something." He reaches under the counter. "Something special."

In that moment, there isn't a doubt in Jesse's mind that the doctor is going to pull up a forty-five-caliber revolver and kill him on the spot, there in the store that's empty but for the two of them. Instead the Brit brings up a 45 rpm record in a plain white sleeve. "Don't review them there single recordings," croaks Jesse, "not my particular line."

"Mate!" Winston says in his flat nasal voice, hurt. "And here I gone to all the trouble of setting it aside for ya. I won't hear of you not taking it," he insists, "I believe you owe it to yourself and to music fans everywhere to give it a spin and let us know *exactly what you think.*"

Grateful enough for not having been shot and wanting to get out of the shop as quickly as he can, Jesse approaches the counter, reaches for the record in whatever manner will keep the other man as much at arm's length as possible, and snatches it from the countertop. Once outside the store and down the street, he tosses the record into a corner trash can before stopping frozen a block away, where he has a funny feeling.

Winston

Within minutes, maybe even moments of Jesse's departure from the record store, Winston quits the job—although no one else is there for him to quit to—and walks out, the shop unlocked and unattended behind him. Were he to not turn the opposite direction outside the door, he might pass the trash can in which Jesse has tossed what Winston gave him; he might bump into Jesse standing there frozen with his funny feeling on the sidewalk.

By the time his marriage broke up back in Hamburg, there wasn't a day when Winston didn't hit her. For a while he told himself, as such men do, that she was asking for it, with her merciless taunts from bed of *Doctor O'Boogie lost his woogie?*—when did her English get so bloody clever?—but that was before sex stopped being a theoretically viable prospect altogether, impotence giving way to nothing more complicated than pure hostility.

In earlier days, before and during and after his band's brief popular streak in Europe, the death of her first husband was a bond between them, all the more because that husband was his best friend. It was something for them to get over together, as he put it to her: "It's simple, really. We decide to survive together or mourn separately," and this seemed to resemble, as much as anything, the makings of a marriage if not love.

Then the grief wore off, as it was supposed to. When her photography career went the way of his record sales and their efforts to have a child were no more successful, she got a job as a barmaid at his favorite watering hole, which meant he drank somewhere else, which he took as liberty to drink twice as much, which he took as liberty to beat her twice as often. Occasioned by his usual verbal and physical belligerence toward the arresting officers, he was nabbed by German police in a small neighborhood grocery store shoplifting his favorite chocolate wafers. She was too bruised and battered to show up at his deportation, not wanting to cause him more trouble than he already had made for himself, or to convince authorities they should throw him in jail rather than out of the country, where she wanted him.

Back in London, a momentary rapprochement with his former musical partner also came to blows. Seeing little point in returning to Liverpool, in seven months he was in the States, where, for a while, he had what appeared to be a promising career as a cartoonist freelancing for various newspapers and journals. This included a recently launched jazz magazine in which, to his grim amusement, he found himself mentioned by his true archnemesis—the shadow of his unlived future—whom he would meet one more time in the record shop on Macdougal when the cartooning career predictably dissolved in a series of editorial scuffles. Another twelve years would follow of one odd job after another, the last as doorman of an apartment at Seventy-Second and Central Park West.

The building is named for once having been considered to be as bleakly secluded from the rest of Manhattan Island in the 1880s as are the Badlands from the rest of America in the twenty-first century. At his post, Winston watches enter and exit movie stars, playwrights, and financiers who predate any America in which Jesse has survived in place of his twin. The doorman spots in the park across the street the predators of fame, would-be assassins; he would know them anywhere. Each is his own twin. Unable to stand the parade of celebrity and accomplishment in and out of the building, Winston roots for those hiding in the trees, conspires with them in silence.

Finally from the apartment building's archway shadows one December night, he attacks an eighty-seven-year-old actress who
began making motion pictures in 1912, her most famous role that
of a Southern belle molested by a black man in a silent Civil War
epic, her honor salvaged only by the Ku Klux Klan on their thun-
dering midnight ride for racial righteousness. The British expat
spends the next twenty years in and out of jail, in and out of Sal-
vation Army centers, in and out of homeless shelters on nights
when he's lucky. Slunk against the base of skyscraper centers, hair
and beard grown jesusian wild, he simultaneously begs for spare
change and verbally abuses passersby.

Struggling to his feet, "Fookin' peasants," he rails, pedestrians
scurrying as though he's just exploded, "far as I can see." As he
mutter-slobbers on the sidewalk, his delirium would seem to
consume not only his own reason but that of anyone within earshot, until his final hours ten mornings before the fall—in the
first year following the century that he was supposed to change
but didn't—when, from his place on the city corner that he's come
to claim, he has what in one last act of reason he insists to himself
is a dream.

But it isn't. Eyes full of the southwestern sky, he watches a Boeing airliner head straight for the northern twin of the tallest structure he's seen, only to swerve at the last moment, missing the Tower and turning westward back to its prescribed destination. Others around him take note as well. "Did you see that?" asks a young woman at his feet. "Looked like that plane just missed . . ." and then, most curiously, sixteen minutes later it appears to happen again, another Boeing swooping toward and avoiding the other Tower. "A flight pattern change?" someone speculates, because what else could explain it?

By the time this vision of aeronautic freakishness bubbles up to the evening news, and though his body hasn't moved, Winston will have gone to what only can be imagined: unfulfillment in the husk of a dreamer's despair. "Did you see that?" the woman on the sidewalk asks again, staring at the Towers; then, glancing around, decides she's talking to herself but for the homeless man slouching against the wall. The woman's name is Pamela, and there on the curb, still pointed in the direction of the Towers, she folds her arms around her as if to hold in some part of herself.

just believe in

After this, it will take her a while, days or maybe weeks, to realize the strange sensation that increasingly comes over her every time she looks at her gynecologist husband, Scott, somehow is related to the sight that September morning of the airliners barely missing the Towers. After this, her husband seems a shadow to her; sometimes she has this funny, funny feeling that he's vanishing by the moment. Eventually she believes he isn't there at all. In the mornings on her way uptown to Macy's, where she works in human resources, Pamela will suddenly stop and turn southwest with the funny, funny feeling that somehow the Towers will be gone too. She barely remembers a British man who worked in the Trade Center for a risk management firm, whatever that is, with whom she once nearly had a moment but for a song that they never heard or danced to, in a time and place where and when no one sang it.

In the twilight that falls and the neon that rises around him, in the growing rush of people beginning to return home from work and brushing past him on their way to the West Fourth Street subway, Jesse stops frozen on the sidewalk. "I got me," he can only mutter out loud, "a funny, funny feeling," waiting for it to pass.

Half a minute he stands immobile there on West Fourth, waiting for the feeling to pass. Then he returns to the corner trash can from where he snatches—as he did from the shop countertop—the record in the plain white sleeve that Winston gave him. He returns to his hotel room where, on the only small table that Jesse has, lies the 45 to which he pays no attention that day or the next, or the next week or the week after.

Not a single time that Jesse passes the 45 sitting on his small table does he bring himself to look at it. But he always knows it's there; months go by. When he moves rooms in his hotel, he packs the 45 in the plain white sleeve with whatever other possessions he has, and when he unpacks the 45, he places it on a shelf facing him that he continues not to look at. A year goes by in New York City and then another.

The 45 is as constant as the dream from which Jesse wakes, the dream of the Tower rooftop and the insurgent night. There isn't a sleeping moment when he isn't returned to the roof, there isn't a dreaming moment that isn't a leap into frosted light a hundred ten stories off the ground. He always wakes in hope that the 45 sitting on the shelf will be gone; he always has a funny feeling when he opens his eyes and the 45 is still there. The years pass and New York is caught in an endless autumn when, one evening, there comes a knock on Jesse's door. He hasn't seen her in a long time. "Hello, darling," Candy says when he answers, "may I die here please?"

"I have a twin," she murmurs on her last night, resolved to expire beautifully with roses on the sheets and twilight in the window, "just like you, cowpoke." Jesse pretends he doesn't hear. She says, "Did you hear me?"

"I surely heard you, darlin'," Jesse at her bedside murmurs back.

"Named Jimmy," but they both figure that her twin isn't like his twin. "My twin isn't like yours," she sighs from the gorgeous glisten of her lymphoma, the makeup that's been so carefully applied pouring off her to reveal the twin beneath, "I am my own twin," to which Jesse answers so quietly that he can't hear himself over the clamor of Village traffic outside, "What makes you think I'm not?" When she's gone, he sits a long time staring below her corpse's waist, deciding whether to finally raise the sheet and look. "What's been down in them parts of you all this time," he asks, still in a whisper so as not to disturb her demise, "Candy or Jimmy?" and then, rather than finally uncover the secret once and for all, he rises from his chair, walks over, and takes the 45 from the shelf. He pulls the single from the sleeve. On the label, the company is listed, just above the hole in the center, as Luna Recording. There is no designated "A" or "B" side, just two titles and the artist's name.

"O Souverain" / "Oh Shenandoah"
Elvis Presley

four

desamor

The first song begins in the early forties as "That's the Blues, Old Man," recorded by an alto sax player nicknamed Jeep with the purest tone anyone ever played on the instrument. By the early fifties, the riff is converted into a modest hit, and twenty years after the original, the definitive version is made by one of the two or three most important artists in the history of rhythm and blues, the "hardest-working man in show business" and "godfather of soul," designations self-invented and beyond dispute anyway. *All aboard!* calls the song over more or less Jeep's same riff, punctuating an itinerary—Miami, Atlanta, Raleigh, DC, Richmond, and don't forget New Orleans, home of the blues, until, finally, *carry me home*—for every train in American music: the mystery train and the midnight train to Georgia, but most of all the train that's coming so people get ready. This is the train that rolls out of black churches into white radios. This is the train of deliverance but also the one where there's nowhere to hide, the train that every American takes to the end of the line, the same shadow-railroad of history that moved black Southern slaves to the free North in the first half of the nineteenth century. The second song's composer, one of rhythm and blues' finest guitarists, feels commanded by God to write the song, and for his sacred effort God rewards him by dropping a lighting rig on him at a concert one summer evening in Brooklyn. He never walks or plays again, singing this song for the rest of his life lying flat on his back on the studio floor.

devices of experience

Things don't just disappear into thin air, Parker and Zema's father has heard his whole life. But if he has existed to prove anything, it's that this isn't true. Toward the end, he's come to realize that things in his life always disappear into thin air, before it's his life itself that begins disappearing: all those eyeglasses by which to see things, those headphones by which to hear things, wallets by which to identify himself, all those devices of experience that he's attached to himself or gripped in his hands and that so pointedly have disappeared, that so pointedly have vanished from his fingers and his eyes and ears, from his memory, to which he has committed the things that—by such devices—he believes he has learned.

Late at night, after the rest of the family was asleep, Parker and Zema's father would tend his playlists like people tend their gardens. As other men's fantasies run to harems or world power, he is the Supreme Sequencer ensconced on a mountaintop or at the edge of a cobalt grove with his catacomb of songs in their proper place, his archive of sequences that he sets right—not among mediocre song-collections, since no one cares about those, but recorded masterpieces with the flaws that make them human. The problem with musicians, the father seethes, is that they're not novelists; they have no sense of narrative. Didn't the saloon singer understand he should open, not end, his torch-song cycle with "One for My Baby," setting up the rest as flashback, and then (as the singer himself would grasp years later in concert) close with, not squander near the beginning, "Angel Eyes" with its devastating final line? In short the Supreme Sequencer reorders, which is to say improves—well, why put so fine a point on it?— *perfects* all the greatest long-players ever made. If he himself is incapable of perfection in anything he does as a father or writer (not to mention that he can't sing or play a note), at least he manages musical perfection's finishing touches.

His wife used to joke to their friends that when it came to parenting Parker and Zema, the mother and father weren't so much good cop and bad cop as horrible cop and no cop. *Funny line*, he would fume silently at the suggestion that he was absent when it came to the responsibilities of raising their children. But while it was true that he held a laissez-faire philosophy on certain things, that he felt it was up to his son and daughter to find their own way on smaller matters such as the existence of Satan or Republicans, like any good father he attempted to set them straight on more fundamental verities from which he knew mob hysteria conspired to sway them. "Now, kids," he said at one such evening convocation around the family dining table, choosing his words so as not to alarm them unduly, filled with the misery of any father who imparts tragic dimensions of life and thereby sullies innocence with reality at its harshest and most despicable, "I know this will be difficult to comprehend, but you're at an age when there are certain things you need to know."

Mustering moral authority, he choked, "I need you to listen to me so as to be mindful when forces of darkness attempt to lead you astray. Try to understand that someone who thinks Queen and the Grateful Dead are good"—this caused him a particular pang, since their mother was known to have a fondness for the former band—"is not necessarily a bad person. Sometimes," he allowed, "good people can believe bad things. But then there are purists, elitists if you will, cultural clergy," indignation rising, "who will tell you that mono is better than stereo, for instance.

There are those in the audiophiliac oligarchy who will tell you that vinyl is better than MP3s. Well, we're not reactionaries in this family, goddamn it—"

"Okay," his wife interjected.

"—we're democrats, egalitarians. We're futurists, we don't go back. *Pet Sounds* is *not* better in fucking mono."

"All right," she admonished.

"*Blonde on Blonde* is not better in mono. Do you understand what I'm saying, kids?" Sixteen-year-old Parker seemed slightly stunned (was he smoking weed again?), eight-year-old Zema was wide-eyed. "As for MP3s, not only can I carry *all* my songs on *this*," he said, holding up his cell, "I can put them in the *correct order* that the artists in their so-called fucked-up genius—"

Sighing, his wife stood from the table, retrieving her car keys. "Let's," she said to the boy and girl, "go for a drive, shall we? Give your father some alone time."

"Stereo," their father continued, following them out the front door to the driveway, "is the sound of America. Open! Wide! Containing multitudes. MP3s," striding alongside the departing car until he worked up to a sprint, "are the format of the twenty-first century. Unmoored! Restless! Perfectible. Don't forget that, kids," he called to the car's red rear lights disappearing down the road, the howl of canyon coyotes rising around him, "and don't," he shouted after his wife, "ever say I didn't teach them something *important*."

disappearing (the world-famous author)

When he was young, reflexively he resisted the music of his time out of what he now realizes was pathological nonconformity to what everyone around him embraced. He pretended that teen anthems were beneath him while secretly he remained glued to the car radio on summer afternoons when he was hired to water neighbors' lawns. Unconsciously yet unmistakably his Damascene conversion was timed exactly with moving out of his parents' house. As well, the music became inextricable from the paroxysms of his country. Did his country lead him to the music or did the music lead him to his country? Now, as close to the end of his life as he then was to the beginning, there are song-moments, song-statistics he recalls more vividly than the disappearing names of best friends. When he discovers that he himself is disappearing with his memories, when he gazes around and grasps pieces of his world going missing, when he peers down and finds pieces of himself missing, he realizes it has been going on awhile; it has been going on for *years*. It has been going on at least since he became world famous, although he can't remember exactly when that was, since he has come to feel he always has been world famous, even as he suspects this isn't the case. In any event, his world fame has become pervasive and all-consuming enough that one of the vanished memories is what it was like *not* to have been world famous.

what you need, you have to borrow

Painfully aware of how people gawk at him when he walks down the street, of the rising murmur at cocktail parties when he walks in the room, finally he has fled to this city at the nation's far northeastern corner, as far as possible from the southwestern corner that is his home. By his burden of world fame, he has been driven to the opposite end of a secret highway that cuts through the heart of the country from one end to the other with impunity. Not entirely clear how long he's been here, the world-famous author arrived when the Surrogates no longer were a sufficient answer to his dilemma of notoriety. He first assembled the Surrogates in the months immediately following publication of his last novel, as his world fame crested; while he most wants to emulate those authors he so admires who shun the spotlight and allow their work to speak for itself, the demands of world fame of the scope and scale that approximate his don't allow for this luxury. Those other authors, he realizes, may be famous but not *world* famous. Originally the Surrogates numbered four. Then he added another and then another when world fame permeated readership south of the border. That left two for the States and Canada, two for Europe, and one for Japan before it occurred to him, waking one night in some dismay, that one for Japan couldn't possibly be enough, that he needed at least two or three for Japan alone. He's big in Japan, the Cheap Trick of American fiction.

disappearing (the surrogates)

The Surrogates all had code names like Secret Service agents. They all shared the world-famous author's lack of any particularly vivid personality, which is to say they were bland enough to pass for him, barring close inspection. All were about his age. Well, more or less his age. Well, some were about ten years younger. Twenty years. All of them, actually. Then the Surrogates began disappearing as well, into the wilds of South America and northern Africa, disappearing or maybe just resigning or retiring, maybe escaping, until there were only two left, whose code names were Search & Destroy and One Nation Under a Groove. As it happened, the two remaining Surrogates were identical twins. Or maybe that wasn't a coincidence, maybe one stayed because the other did. Dispatched in the world-famous author's stead to book tours and radio-show appearances and soirees of offended female readers—who might have been mollified by the fact that, seen from a certain angle, the Surrogates bore some resemblance to a world-famous singer, in fact the most famous singer who ever lived, to whom the world-famous author bears no resemblance in the least—soon one or the other was going off the reservation, shall we say? Somewhat outrageous quotes were uttered. Provocatively borderline behavior was committed.

This was a problem not because of the outrageousness itself of the quotes, or the provocation itself of the behavior, but because those who know the world-famous author, to the extent that anyone does, realize that he never utters anything outrageous or does anything provocative, and therefore Search & Destroy and One Nation Under a Groove can't possibly be him and are thereby revealed as impostors. With a start, the world-famous author realizes that the reason other authors shun the spotlight and let their work speak for itself is so that they can *shun the spotlight and let their work speak for itself.* But even in the midst of his world fame, there are obvious ways that he has been disappearing over time. In the throes of his celebrity, his *phenomenon*, his work not only becomes of less pertinence but begins to unexist altogether. Whole passages of his work (which of course is about *everything*) evaporate from between the bindings. Then the disappearing becomes more personal, until it's a matter of his life unliving itself. With greater frequency he is confronted by eyewitness accounts of what naively he regards as his past's key occasions or incidents, moments in which he has been under the illusion that he played a crucial role, only to find he played no part whatsoever.

Conversations within plain hearing in which there is any reference to him grow fewer. People within earshot speak more as though he isn't there, and then as though he never has been there, and then as though he never has been. Maybe this is the source of his new dread, or maybe he just has been living so long with more reasonable dread, once supported by more reasonable anxieties, that dread is all he knows. Beginning around the time when Zema came home at the age of two, the family went through an almost biblically difficult seven years, and if they emerged more or less intact on the other side—maybe it's around then that he became world famous? Or was it before, unlikely as that seems?— they weren't unscathed. In the process, Parker and Zema's father learned that he is a man of only shakable integrity at best (whatever that means, one might ask, but not him). He so vested his trust in ongoing and relentless crisis that he came to trust little else. Now, writing these words one gray twilight in the farthest northeast corner of the country, he finds time disappearing around him, not necessarily all time or everyone else's, just his own. As he watches now from his window in the Sonark with the New Dublin boulevard rolling before him, the sun flickers on and off as though increments of its trajectory are atomizing themselves in the heavens. At first he figures he's just getting his quadrants confused, his norths mixed up with his easts.

quadrex

Like all Americans, or like all Americans who are conscious of being American, Parker and Zema's father always believed he *was* his country. But lately he's come to realize that if he and his family didn't emerge unscathed from their American crisis, American faith in the early part of the twenty-first century didn't emerge at all. By the conclusion of the new century's first score of years, only those who have a stake in an American idea defined by wealth and power can still speak of that idea so shamelessly, since wealth and power is the only American idea left. If the evil of the attacks on that September morning could be set aside, and of course it could not, nothing better presented America with the opportunity to reimagine itself. This was an opportunity at once botched and fulfilled, with, on the one hand, a war of worse faith than anything the country has done in a hundred years, and by the election on the other hand of a man the color of African orphans—all followed by hope's collapse. Yet the father can't shake his obsession with his country even in the face of his country's disappearance, in the same way that he can't shake his obsession with himself in the face of his own disappearance. Now the world-famous author has come to a place where American daylight is on the run.

On the run, American daylight arrives a couple of hours before noon and departs just a few hours after, black gulls from the sea swooping into the city like bats. Taking his room in the curve of the Sonark at the far end of Abyssinthe Road, the world-famous author can see from his large window that wraps around the building the college in the distance and the lattice of winter-woven trees beyond which lies the Atlantic. Traffic surges and ebbs up and down the boulevard. A steady stream of students enters and exits the taverns and café where he gets muffins on black mornings, and like land's hot air smashing the cold of the sea into fog, space's sonic rain beats the silence of the city floor into a silver *shhh*. A woman in her midtwenties plays guitar on the sidewalk below, although no cup or cap or open guitar case at her feet receives the tribute of passersby. He thinks maybe she's familiar to him. She has dark cropped hair and a scar on her nose where a ring used to be. "What is a sonark anyway?" she asks one afternoon when he walks by, and the world-famous author explains that as a lighthouse is a beacon in the dark, a sonark is a beacon in the silence. Studying the tower behind him, the guitarist frowns. "If it's a beacon in the silence, I don't hear it making any sound," she says, and he answers, indicating her guitar, "Maybe you're the sound."

track 15:

"Surrender"

but don't give yourself away.

During his stay at the Sonark, the world-famous author persists in believing that one morning he finally will complete the line that he's arrived in New Dublin to finish:

Here come the planes, so you better—

Run? hide? scream? You better die? You better . . . what? All the possibilities seem obvious, and yet he feels sure that the correct conclusion is inclusive of the others, meaning something that doesn't choose running or hiding at the exclusion of screaming or dying. He also has a nagging suspicion that he knows this line from Another Place or Time. He worries that it's something he already has written; then one morning he wakes realizing, to his enormous chagrin, that the line is from a song, and that he's come all this way to finish a line that isn't even his, not just written by someone else but sung for millions to hear. Since he has made it a habit to leave pulled open at night the curtains of his room so that the city lights splash across his closed eyelids when he dreams, he can't rule out that the song has come through the window as well.

towers of song (new doubling)

On his laptop at his fingertips, as he gazes out over Abyssinthe Road from his window and can hear up and down the thoroughfare the *shhh* misting in from the side streets, he has twin playlists of a hundred and ten songs, each drawn from a musical library of 2,996. Of course, as music's Supreme Sequencer he has systemized the playlists precisely according to a rationale that's evident to him if no one else:

Générique	Ethanopium
Crosstown Traffic	The Sky Is Crying
Ghost Riders in the Sky	Armenia City in the Sky
Tombstone Shadow	Paradise Circus
Rebel Girl	Route 66
Slip Inside This House	Ballrooms of Mars
Parachute Woman	Paper Planes
Airborne	Atomic
What a Good Man He Is	Papa Don't Take No Mess
Little Babies	Family Affair
Piece of My Heart	Get Ur Freak On
Can You Get to That	Can I Get a Witness
Comet Melody 2	First Cool Hive
My Kingdom	Erase You
If You Were a Bluebird	If It Be Your Will
Marquee Moon	Planet Rock
Seven Nation Army	Eight Miles High
Dancing in the Dark	Spirit in the Dark

Bring the Noise	Paid in Full
Lonesome Fugitive	Nowhere to Run
That Lucky Old Sun	Warmth of the Sun
Venus in Furs	Virgin Beauty
Black Coffee	Lush Life
Higher Ground	Body and Soul
Hot Burrito	Sue Egypt
Mannish Boy	Freddie's Dead
Ain't No More Cane	Sign o' the Times
I Cover the Waterfront	Then He Kissed Me
Minnie the Moocher	Mustang Sally
Stop Breaking Down	Personality Crisis
Moonlight Drive	The Passenger
Boom Boom	Wooly Bully
Rebellion (Lies)	Teen Age Riot
Back Stabbers	Stagger Lee
Rockaway Beach	Neptune City
Bernadette	Lucille
Snow White Diner	Wichita Lineman
Oh Shenandoah	O Superman
St. James Infirmary	Psychedelic Shack
Lose Yourself	I Feel Love
96 Tears	Hey Ya
Jockey Full of Bourbon	Straight, No Chaser
Theme from *Now, Voyager*	Theme from *Peter Gunn*
Smoke Gets in Your Eyes	You Go to My Head
Bad Reputation	All Apologies
My Funny Valentine	This Bitter Earth
Ballad of El Goodo	Song to the Siren
Summertime	Winterlong
Stardust	Debaser
Pyramid Song	Redemption Song

and so on . . .

the secret track's secret track

. . . and so on the morning when he wakes to the realization that the unfinished line is from a song, he tries to hum it, or to hum what is behind the words that he hears in his head, not realizing that in this particular song, these particular words aren't actually sung but spoken, and there's only the barest melody.

Here come the planes, so you better . . .

he singsong-says to himself over and over, thinking he'll finish the line instinctively, half-melody hovering in his mind at the edge of recognition while he sits for hours by the window watching people and cars . . .

... in the road below, airplanes in the sky as rare as rain. But he can't place the song no matter how hard he racks his brain— and then one morning, when, as always, he wakes to the line in his head, almost in an instant he realizes that the song is on one of his twin playlists that he has listened to over the previous months and years. With mounting excitement, he returns to the lists. . . .

Générique	Ethanopium
Crosstown Traffic	The Sky Is Crying
Ghost Riders in the Sky	Armenia City in the Sky
Tombstone Shadow	Paradise Circus
Rebel Girl	Route 66
Slip Inside This House	Ballrooms of Mars
Parachute Woman	Paper Planes
Airborne	Atomic
What a Good Man He Is	Papa Don't Take No Mess
Little Babies	Family Affair
Piece of My Heart	Get Ur Freak On
Can You Get to That	Can I Get a Witness
Comet Melody 2	First Cool Hive
My Kingdom	Erase You
If You Were a Bluebird	If It Be Your Will
Marquee Moon	Planet Rock
Seven Nation Army	Eight Miles High
Dancing in the Dark	Spirit in the Dark

Bring the Noise

Lonesome Fugitive

That Lucky Old Sun

Venus in Furs

Black Coffee

Higher Ground

Hot Burrito

Mannish Boy

Ain't No More Cane

I Cover the Waterfront

Minnie the Moocher

Stop Breaking Down

Moonlight Drive

Boom Boom

Rebellion (Lies)

Back Stabbers

Rockaway Beach

Bernadette

Snow White Diner

Oh Shenandoah

St. James Infirmary

Lose Yourself

96 Tears

Jockey Full of Bourbon

Theme from *Now, Voyager*

Smoke Gets in Your Eyes

Bad Reputation

My Funny Valentine

Ballad of El Goodo

Summertime

Stardust

Pyramid Song

Paid in Full

Nowhere to Run

Warmth of the Sun

Virgin Beauty

Lush Life

Body and Soul

Sue Egypt

Freddie's Dead

Sign o' the Times

Then He Kissed Me

Mustang Sally

Personality Crisis

The Passenger

Wooly Bully

Teen Age Riot

Stagger Lee

Neptune City

Lucille

Wichita Lineman

Psychedelic Shack

I Feel Love

Hey Ya

Straight, No Chaser

Theme from *Peter Gunn*

You Go to My Head

All Apologies

This Bitter Earth

Song to the Siren

Winterlong

Debaser

Redemption Song

. . . only to realize with a glance . . .

. . . because it takes only a glance for it to be instantly apparent, that the second playlist now is shorter than the first. One of the songs is gone. The Supreme Sequencer stares at the once-twin playlists assuming there's a mistake; it must be, he tries to convince himself, that the second list isn't shorter but that the first is longer because maybe a title accidentally has been duplicated? since, after all, songs don't just disappear into thin air. But the moment that he considers this, some part of him knows better, some part of his brain that has mapped these compilations so as to immediately recognize something is amiss even when he can't tell what, some part of him that can discern havoc has been wrought and the order of the playlist violated even as he can't pinpoint the violation. He stares hard at the second list, concentrating, subliminally identifying—in his sequencing supremacy—that the sequence has gone awry somewhere near the bottom. But with a horror more acute than all of his various vanishings have instilled so far, he concludes his sequences are vanishing too.

Sitting before his curved window, he peers at the floor around him. He checks the pockets of his coat hanging on the back of his chair. In alarm, he glances at the sill just beyond the window—where he keeps a carton of milk in the winter chill as refrigeration—in case the song has, like a cat, crawled too far out. For a moment he feels certain that he catches a glimpse of the song bolting down the street, calling to strangers for help. *You always were free to go as you chose*, he thinks indignantly, *never my prisoner*; but he's not sure this is true. He wonders if this is the onset of a full-fledged revolt. He looks at the lists again to determine if any of the others have made a break, if they're congregating in mutinous groups, punk tribes and psychedelic clans, bebop cabals and rhythm-and-blues secret societies. If he's being honest, he knows the reason for his congenital eclecticism is to keep the songs isolated from fellow like-spirited songs and thereby powerless: in their heterogeneity lies his control. One afternoon he's convinced that he spots from his window the song skittering into the guitar of the young woman in the street, lurking in the instrument's hollow. But when he pulls on his clothes and rushes down the circular stairs, she's gone by the time he reaches the bottom.

and when force is gone, there's always

Upon first checking into the Sonark, having seen the wraparound window from the street below and known it was the room where he was meant to finish his work, he's been slightly surprised by his own demands, not having thought of himself as demanding. But these are the perks of world fame, and thus is his dedication to completing the line in his head and thus is his resolve to uncover whatever it is that better be done because the planes are coming. Having searched the city—which, considering he never heard of New Dublin before he became world famous, he finds shockingly grand for an American city, with palatial promenades and arching bridges and vast parks and the centuries-old campus built around the old settlement's remnants—he takes the room for a month on the condition that the Sonark move out some of the furniture, a qualification about which he's politely adamant in the face of the concierge's resistance. Since checking in, he has persevered in rearranging the room further, shifting an armoire from one end to the other; had he a sledgehammer in hand, he would knock out one of the walls. So when he wakes in the middle of the night hearing the song in the ceiling above, nothing is going to stop him from chasing it down.

He can't be sure if the song is hiding or trapped. It trills at him softly that night and the next, and then more faintly. *It's on the move!* and to the concierge's consternation, the following morning he insists on transferring to the room above. "Please, sir," she cries, "we can't be rearranging more furniture!" Then that night in the upstairs room he hears the song in the wall mocking him, and the next morning he demands to be moved next door. Several nights later—or has it been longer than that?—he has chased the song up the cylindrical core of the Sonark, realizing that the wayward lyric has grown less distinct, not more. One ravished room after another around the pillar's perimeter lies in his wake. Night after night he thrashes in bed to the swirling of the song's harmonizer, as the city lights ripple like a strobe across his closed eyelids. Winding upward, the world-famous author curves his way around until he's on the other side and the city is out of sight altogether. With the curtains of his window pulled open as usual while he "sleeps," the streetlights that flashed across his eyelids are replaced by the moon's glint off the cobalt domes of the far grove.

Unable to complete the line of the song, the world-famous author has the shocking revelation that he always has been better at any stage of incompletion than in any state of final completeness. He realizes that at the incomplete moment he always has the potential to be better than he ends up actually being. He's shocked to realize that nothing he has ever finished has been as good as it was moments before he finished it. A playlist consists of not only the songs that are on it but those left off for reasons having nothing to do with whether a song is good or bad, because addition of the wrong song disrupts the haunting of songs left incomplete by their missing twins. When the Towers came down in September 2001, he spent the following days composing a playlist that would properly unlock a flabbergasting new century. As the twentieth century was about politics, which is to say survival, the twenty-first is about God, which is to say oblivion, a subject his country is profoundly unprepared to contemplate. He found there wasn't a single song worthy of the event or undiminished by it, or that didn't diminish the event in return. No song proved at once big and intimate enough, after the world-famous author spent a lifetime believing there always is a song big or intimate enough.

With the buildings, all the songs crumpled into rubble, all the songs born of a failed dream that marked the century before and the century before that. The world-famous author was left only to hope that if no one song held the key to comprehension, then a playlist might encompass enough meaning for a new century's birth in flame and blood, beginning with the 1931 version of "All of Me" by a Storyville hooker's jazz-jesus son whose sense of self-myth was keen and unreliable enough for him to claim he was born on the Fourth of July 1900. The playlist finished with a 1999 song called "The Sky Is Broken," by the white Harlem-born technautic distant descendent of a world-famous author who located American obsession in the form of a white sea-bound monster. Between exhaustion and sleep, humiliated by the growing suspicion that he's not world-famous after all and maybe never has been, Parker and Zema's father wanders the archive of the Sonark interrupted now and then by small portholes through which can be seen Outside's rolling knolls. Dappled lunar light splatters the tufts of trees. Imperceptibly the mass of the music lining the archive corridors shifts form, songs in one place vibrating themselves to another.

Rambling down his hall of playlists, Parker and Zema's father glimpses memory in every song-portal, reaching the corridor's end without locating the song that tells him what he better do when the planes come. Rather he stumbles on a nameless scratch of mellotron where, sticking his head inside to climb through and poised to cross its threshold, he's surrounded by future-reverie, the not-before-seen but remembered anyway. Over the flat silvery mesa of the ambientphonik shines an enormous orb so ashen he can't be sure if it's an eclipsed sun or a full moon, in the grim light of which two massive open graves gape in the distance, earth-wounds transported from national recollection. Crouched before the twin graves, two tiny figures grow larger as he draws closer to them. The world-famous author can't help feeling fucking annoyed. "Oh well," he says in a huff as they unfold themselves and rise to their feet, "nice of you two to show up. Finally."

Search & Destroy sighs heavily, turns to One Nation Under a Groove. "You want to tell him?" he asks, and for a moment the other Surrogate regards the world-famous author sadly. "Listen," he says at last.

The least violent of men, the world-famous author has a notion, overwhelming to an extent that startles him, to take a good pop at One Nation Under a Groove and knock him into the pit behind. "What?" he snaps instead, stopping in his tracks. "I suppose you're going to tell me I'm not world famous."

The Surrogate shakes his head. "You're not."

"Then what do I need you for?"

"You don't," and the world's least-famous author peers up at the rumbling sky and its orb the color of cinder, then down at the scorched cavities of the Towers. "Where is this?" he mutters. "These don't belong here." He nods at the graves. "I saw them come down on TV, it didn't happen anywhere around here, wherever this . . . is. . . ." He says, "Everything changed when they came down."

"Oh lord," moans Search & Destroy, rolling his eyes, "not the 'everything changed' thing."

"The world-famous part, just so you know?" says One Nation Under a Groove. "That's *not* one of the things that changed."

"I feel sure," the world's barely known author starts to protest, "that I was *going* to be world fa—"

"It was never in the cards. Get over yourself."

"We all want to believe everything changed," says Search &

Destroy, "but really? *Everything went back to normal*, or what was *really* normal, given that we never were as impervious to the chaos of human history as we thought."

"I . . . wrote about all this!" sputters the author. "How the twentieth century—"

"Oh, sure," says One Nation Under a Groove, "we've all been hanging on every word, too." Search & Destroy bursts into laughter and soon both Surrogates are laughing. "Twentieth century this, America that. You call this change?" he says, gesturing at everything around them. "This was just mixing up the name tags, dude. You're sitting at the bride's table one minute, the groom's the next."

"Man," chortles Search & Destroy, indicating himself and the other, "even the *fake* you's are smarter than the real you. What's *that* tell you? By the way"—he reaches into his back pocket—"here's what you've been looking for."

Parker and Zema's father takes from the Surrogate a silver disc, blank but for a scrawl in black marker across its face that includes the name of the world-famous singer to whom the Surrogates bear some resemblance and to whom the author bears none in the least. He tries to make out the song title in the ashy light of the moon. "Who can read this? 'Oh Shadowbahn'?"

"'Shenandoah.' Nineteenth-century American folk—"

"I know 'Oh Shenandoah,'" he snaps, looking at the singer's name, "but I never knew *he* recorded it. Anyway," he insists, "I don't think this tells me what I better do when the planes come."

"Oh, that," the Surrogate assures him. "That's the flip side."

Meanwhile. More than three decades before "Night Train" becomes a hit, a slave's grandson who borrows Jeep's sax riff for a work called *Deep South Suite*—and who also writes "Mood Indigo" and "Solitude" and "Sophisticated Lady" and "Take the A Train" and "Prelude to a Kiss" and "Day Dream" and "Isfahan" and "Transblucency" and "Moon Mist" and "It Don't Mean a Thing If It Ain't Got That Swing"—makes his first of nearly a dozen recordings of "Black and Tan Fantasy," in which lurks a magnum opus. It's the soundtrack of Harlem's Cotton Club at its most riotous and becomes the basis of a twenty-minute RKO film with an entirely black cast. A man of grace and, perhaps, perspective, the composer has the class and, perhaps, irony to congratulate a younger next-generation pianist for being on the cover of the country's most prominent weekly newsmagazine, to which the abashed young pianist can only stammer, "It should have been you," acknowledging ever after that only because he's white is he on the cover in place of the older, black maestro. (He will write a song in his hero's honor called "The Duke.") "Black and Tan Fantasy" is part witty funeral march interspersed with a twilit summer stroll down Lenox Avenue, as though the body, on its way to an eternal resting place in a Harlem cemetery, lets loose its spirit for one last jaunt around the neighborhood. In the short movie, a beautiful young cabaret performer dances herself to death during the song. The deep Harlem grave is a portal to forty years later, when a St. Louis dentist's son with a horn leads an expedition to the end of African exile, the far finish of the great Ghanaian and Senegalese scattering, the exodus not from slavery to freedom, as in the Old Testament, but the other way around. "Miles Runs the Voodoo Down" isn't just three centuries of a people's history in fourteen musical minutes marked by wail, smolder, outburst, and flying-dutchman phantasmatoons adrift in the shoals of reef-smashed chords, it's the response from the damned America to the call of that America that might still be redeemed in "Black and Tan Fantasy," as the spirit of America takes off—from its body on its way to being interred—for one last jaunt around all the possibilities that the country once imagined for itself, even as those possibilities were betrayed before the country began. As well, running down the voodoo, the horn player (a man of no small ego, imbued with the fury of having had his brains almost bashed in by police when he's seen in the company of a blonde outside Birdland mere weeks after recording what will go on to become the single most loved jazz album of all time) now pursues and sets to music his own oblivion, the sound of his own nothingness, the sound of something beyond burial. At once intermediary between the two men and successor to them is a third, whose songs are shadows to these two. American mongrel of black, Cherokee, and Irish, raised in Seattle by a family so abusive that a social worker reports only the boy's interest in guitar will save him, he migrates to London, seat of the Old World, proceeding directly to legend bypassing mere notoriety. Seven months after leaving his country in obscurity, he returns with epic ambient-groove soundscapes that move from urban chaos to oceanic grottoes to perilous distant shores that no one can cross, breaking down psychic walls between outer space and inner. The trumpeter hears the guitarist's intergalactic blues with titles like "Third Stone from the Sun" and "Voodoo Chile (Slight Return)," and follows them to where there is no return, slight or otherwise.

Written during the great national crisis of the thirties, both
are answers to the great national crisis of the forties, whose
other songs so palpably and desperately promise "I'll be seeing
you" and "We'll meet again," when no one can bring themselves
to reply, You won't, and We can't, except on some Other Side
of love or life that's either celestial or earthly. The human heart
commits its greatest treachery by healing. It commits its greatest
treachery by surviving the love that was supposed to last forever,
that was supposed to be the heart's burden into eternity, only for
that burden to be laid down by too much time and, worse, too
much banality, too much of everything that's beneath love, not
good enough for love. Though "Stormy Weather" is composed
at the depths of Depression gloom as the New Deal is being
born, its signature recording comes in a year when the country
goes to war, the singer a former Cotton Club chorus-line beauty
who's part black, part white, and part American Indian, a great-
great-granddaughter on her mother's side of John Calhoun,
America's most virulent defender of slavery before the Civil
War. Since its melody is written by a Jewish kid from New
York—like so many other American Songbook authors—who
also writes "Over the Rainbow" and "Come Rain or Come
Shine," it would be logical to assume he has meteorology on the
brain, but he doesn't pen the words (or titles) of any of these
songs, so something in his music with its portents of clouds and
precipitation and shimmer would seem to bring out the climatic

in his three entirely different collaborators. (It might also be noted that the composer is the surviving twin of a brother who died within twenty-four hours of childbirth.) Striking a chord with an America yearning for the "innocence" that subsequent commentators always suggest the country has "lost" but that never was there to begin with, "Where or When" channels the lexicon of recollection that becomes bittersweet only when you're finally as old as I am and your time is marked most by the children who follow, like my children mark mine. "I think," I tried to tell my son once, "that even as the body ages, the psyche settles into whatever was your best moment, the moment when you most came into your own and fulfilled your clearest sense of who you are, when everything about you fell into the best alignment it will ever know" [Parker has no recollection of this conversation, and wouldn't know what his father was talking about in any case]. Maybe it's the same for a country, its psyche clinging to whenever was fulfilled its clearest sense of itself. On Broadway, "Where or When" is originally and inexplicably sung by someone too young to sing such a song. But then, from my increasingly wintry perspective I've come to realize that all the great songs are sung by someone too young, who can't remember that once romantic love, as opposed to a parent's love, seemed so powerful that he thought he could die for it, only to realize in the lengthening shade of the coming end that some such loves nearly have slipped memory altogether. *Seems we stood and talked like this before . . . but I can't remember . . .* All the young singers, what the fuck do they know? But sometimes the songs know more than either the young singers or the young songwriters, those teams of boys writing the Great American Songbook, pairs of young men always from New York writing the great musical album for a white, Manhattan-male nation, writing all they know of a nation's longings and dashed fulfillments—which is to say there's a shadow songbook somewhere, clandestine in plain earshot, written from other parts of the country also in plain earshot, of other genders and colors. When black fifteen-year-old Eleanora Fagan from other-side-of-the-Hudson Philly by way of Baltimore, the daughter of a single unwed mother and undetermined father, sings "I'll Be Seeing You" (from yet another musical written by yet another pair of young New York men), you can hold her singing to the flame of whatever candles flicker at the Alhambra club or Pod's & Jerry's in Harlem and there burns into earshot the words and melody of that other songbook along with the singer's shadow name—Billie—which overtakes her real one like wildfire. She dies in a hospital under arrest, handcuffed to her deathbed, her legend the one thing that can't be taken into custody. Writing and singing these songs while confronting the greatest human conflagration the world has known, was everyone already grown old? Was everyone already weary beyond their years? And what then of the songs on this millennium's birth, that second-to-last Tuesday morning of summer in that first year of the twenty-first century? Is anyone now really old enough to write or sing them?

A couple of months from now, long enough after returning to Upper Saskatchewan that they might almost forget the Twin Towers ever were in the Badlands, or that the couple ever drove the thousand miles to see them, Traci wakes one night to the song that she and her wife heard there. She sits up from her bed in the dark trying to determine where it comes from. It sounds so near as to almost be next to her, she thinks.

Then she realizes that the song *is* next to her, when she looks over at Linda, her head on the pillow and sightless eyes wide open, lips pursed and the song curling from her mouth like smoke. *It really gets bad 'round midnight, memories always start.* In terror, Traci bolts from their bed and to the edge of the room; the song from Linda's mouth isn't in Linda's voice or any voice that Traci recognizes. It has no gender or race. The song is in its own voice.

All the stowaway songs are in their own voices, all the songs that never had their own voices but waited for a singer to give them one. A couple of months from now, the midnight incident will give Traci a funny, funny feeling, when she is capable of feeling anything that isn't dread; the day following the incident, Linda will seem almost the same but not quite, and will seem less the same the next day and the day after. She has been invaded, as have the others, the Pattersons and Ortizes and Ramseys and Hartmans, whose one-year-old mutters surfadelic themes of spaghetti Westerns complete with choral vocals and operatic crescendos and ghostly chimes in the distance. Back in their Alexandria *kism*, not far from the ruins of ancient Memphis, where once ruled the Pharaoh Menes, the Nours listen to their thirteen-year-old daughter sing from her sleep, *I'm a rolling stone all alone and lost, for a life of sin I have paid the cost.* The next day they will take her to a doctor to confirm she is still a virgin. Justin Farber, just turning sixty-four knowing he'll never see sixty-five, wakes himself to *When I got home I found a message on the door . . . burning airlines give you so much more* gurgling inside him. As the song scampers away in the night, he watches himself scamper with it. Parked on Lake Pontchartrain's northern shore with the whistle of a song that's been in her head since the Badlands finally went silent, ex-sheriff Rae Jardin strolls a swampland road that she last walked half a century ago, with her grandfather clutching her hand.

Or she thinks it's the same road, anyway. Sometimes she stops in the humid afternoon gazing around her to be sure; gone from this part of her life for decades, nonetheless she assumed when she got here that the memory of it would be as indisputable as it was behind elevator doors in the ghost Tower from where she's come. She figures the vestigial sounds of rain fallen from the trees' higher leaves to the lower leaves hasn't changed in half a century, and that caught in the higher branches falling to the lower branches will be the same laughter of men. She looks for the tree where it happened, because trees endure not knowing one particular blue sky from another, or a particular waft of wind or a crow's particular caw or a particular crowd of men laughing beneath it, or the particular evil of it all. Somewhere between the Badlands and Louisiana, on Interstate 55 outside Jackson after the incident in Valentine, the sheriff decided she needs to see the tree again; but she never finds it. It's disappeared into thin air. Scouring the swamps that afternoon like someone scouring the graveyard for a tomb, finally she gives up. When she reaches her South Dakota patrol car, for a split second, as though peering through a flashing breach in the national memory, like a man waking on the ninety-third floor and in his first sliver of a moment seeing a Boeing 767 airliner flying straight toward him, the sheriff could swear New Orleans is going up in flames before her.

Twenty years to the day after the appearance of the Towers in the Dakota Badlands—when the event might have passed into the kind of Lourdesian legend attending religious visions but for the fact that twenty-first-century technology has borne witness to it—the Towers will reappear in flashes of sightings confirmed by thousands from Delano to Dallas, from Memphis to Montgomery. Some find this route historically unsettling. Occasionally the Towers are separated by an expanse, such as the ten miles of U.S. 80 that divide them in Selma.

Configuring the accumulated data of the new reappearances with satellite photography, researchers can neither ascertain nor dismiss the pattern that forms a five-latitude musical staff, let alone determine which single sighting might represent the beginning clef. This means that the notes signified by the Towers' appearances all over the country might constitute almost any one of a thousand melodies, any or all of which might predictably be "Oh Shenandoah" but, as it happens, are not. Years are spent trying to decode a composition as revelatory as it is circular. America, however, does not do circular.

$$2t = [c+m]^x$$

As with the original Badlands occurrence, unverified is whether the Towers themselves have actually come and gone, appeared and disappeared, or whether they always have been in place and those who see them are appearing and disappearing in time. A decade later this speculation will be rendered more indeterminate by the most groundbreaking scientific formulation since relativity and mass-energy equivalence, Dr. Vondel Shane's PACER (past-consciousness encoded retention) Theory, by which she proves memory isn't a function of time, as assumed for twelve thousand years, but that time empirically and quantifiably is a function of memory, reversing long-accepted polarities of objectivity and subjectivity.

In what by this point is a growing tradition of political uselessness, some call for "laying plans" to greet the Towers' next manifestation in yet another twenty years, although precisely what plan is to be laid remains unclear. Will a massive net be dropped from the sky to hold the Towers in place once they return? Will the skyscrapers be tasered into acquiescence with an immense surge of electricity? In the meantime America—the America, that is to say, that never looked like anything but what it ever was: a dream—comes to bear less resemblance to itself, until it eludes all recognition.

Regions secede from the nation, states from regions, cities from states. By midcentury the recently formed Arklahoma Christian Conglomerate applies to the World Trade Organization for a patent on "America" under the Trade-Related Intellectual Property (TRIP) agreement. A rage of countersuits is filed by other northwestern-hemispheric entities. Attempting without satisfaction to assess the petitions by typical standards of singularity, functionality, and precedent, the organization's council ultimately gathers representatives for the various claimants in a locked conference room where, stripped of all digital resources, each is posed a question with the understanding that the patent for "America" legitimately belongs to whichever answers correctly: Who recorded "West End Blues" in June 1928?

In fact there are two correct responses, thereby doubling every contestant's chances. Both are provided not by any of the would-be patent holders, who know neither answer, but by a bystander in the room representing Nuovo Abyssinia. Up until relatively recently called Ethiopia, N/A has no interest whatsoever in a patent on "America," which paradoxically imparts to the final verdict greater moral logic, given the council's further determination that, as an idea, "America" has existed since before America, since the beginning of time, when only Abyssinia existed.

The "country" becomes crisscrossed by so-called shadow high-ways that remain the only geography recognized as federal land still subject to national sovereignty. Fifteen thousand miles of such thoroughfares are marked by countless arched bridges, con-structed by squatters—desperate to live on or over whatever part of the landscape can be called America anymore—so close to each other that the roads resemble less open highways than hor-izontal chutes. Sometimes these cults build overnight cities on the highways themselves, risking collision and vehicular slaugh-ter for the privilege of assuming the mystical self-identification "American." Although the cultists are viewed by most with sus-picion, nonetheless other continental occupants gather at the sides of the highways to listen to the music that comes from these makeshift cities. In the dark of night, in any spot of the late coun-try that blasts out all its horizons, the arches of America can be heard in either direction as a series of chiming rings stretching as far as the ear can listen.

The music is unlike any heard by anyone since what once was called the "American century," when the predominant music of that century, so compelling as to have spread beyond America, was the expression of and then rebuttal to America's self-betrayal—when the music was about America regardless of whether it came from America, whether it believed in America, whether it thought of America, whether it spurned or rejected America. The previous century's music knew of America whether anyone knew that it did. At the previous century's root was a blues sung at the moment when America defiled its own great idea, which was the moment that idea was born. It was a blues born of American slavery and made by slavery's children, each evolution swallowing whole what preceded it, blues swallowing minstrelsy, ragtime swallowing blues, jazz swallowing ragtime, Tin Pan Alley swallowing jazz, pop swallowing Tin Pan Alley, rock and roll swallowing pop, hip-hop swallowing rock and roll, hip-hop becoming future-minstrelsy among young whites. In the same way that once the twenty-first century was the future, the predominant music of the future—so compelling as to have spread beyond its own moment—was the expression of and then rebuttal to the future's self-betrayal, the future's defilement of its own possibilities at the instant they became possible, which is to say the instant they were imagined. When the date arrives for the Towers to repeat their now-apparent pattern of bi-decadal manifestation and to reappear forty years AD (After Dakota), they're nowhere to be found. In fact, unknown to everyone, they have returned after all, not more than a hundred and fifty miles from the Badlands, buried half a mile beneath the ground on the eastern side of the Missouri River bridge at Chamberlain that was crossed, on the same day that the Towers actualized themselves all those years ago, by the first man to see them.

Portraits of the nation written and recorded within months
of each other in the last twenty years of the twentieth century,
by two singers variously anointed at one time or another
their country's troubadour laureate, its National Voice. But
songs like these weren't what the nation had in mind during
the administration of the half century's most popular and
ruthless president, a political genius who learned before he
ever was in politics that playing an unheroic, ignoble role as
somehow heroic and noble anyway is political genius's first law.
Everywhere you look, life ain't got no soul, goes the first song,
borrowing its lyrical motif from the designated assassins of
thirties and forties organized crime; by the eighties the whole
country was Murder Incorporated, and when the singer nears
the end of the song, the listener realizes that in fact the story's
narrator is dead. The second song is a blues that no one can
sing like Blind Willie McTell, who is not the song's singer and
barely its subject. *Seen the arrow on the doorpost saying this
land is condemned,* these blues begin, and then a minute or
two in, the song's horrors unfold, whips cracking and big
plantations burning. Both songs were mysteriously withheld
from release by their singers in favor of inferior songs, maybe
because none of the other songs could stand association with
two such unforgiving statements. Not twins or brothers, not
father and son (eight years separated them), when they wrote
these songs the singers—Jersey-shore successor to his Midwest

ice-plains predecessor, who was in no mood to be succeeded—
were at opposite ends of their particular arcs. What aesthetic
misjudgments or careerist concerns turned the creation of
these songs into psychodramas for which the only denouement
was the songs' suppression? The successor was on the verge of
being appropriated by a jingoism that he despised even as he
may cannily have understood its expedient uses in terms of his
stardom. The predecessor struggled to emerge from an exile to
which his audience dismissed him less than twenty years after
he became his country's most important white musical figure,
with a mystique so outlandish and improbable that he found it
publicly repellent even as some part of him relished it. The worst
that could be said of the predecessor is that he was an inspired
borrower—so was he unsettled, as he rarely showed evidence
of being, by the unmistakable resemblance of his melody to
another called "St. James Infirmary," about a man who goes
looking for his lost love in what may be a charnel house or
prison or even a brothel like the House of the Rising Sun, only
to find his love cheating on him or incarcerated or dying,
depending on which of countless versions is heard (including
one by the actual Blind Willie McTell)? In any case "Blind
Willie McTell" is so powerful as to momentarily overwhelm
any listener's recollection of its antecedent, and nearly powerful
enough to have overwhelmed the singer's inclinations, wavering
among arrogance and petulance and self-sabotage, to deliver
and render stillborn not just the song but any impact it might
have on his audience's consensus. Consensus is a lynch mob.
Each of the two singers has his lynch mob, with—even as the
successor repeatedly paid homage to the predecessor, who did
nothing less than change the music that the successor came to
save—the predecessor palpably resenting the successor in the
same way that every king resents his prince, and conversely in

the same way that sons declare their independence of fathers. It's hard to know whether my son has any use for either of these supposed laureates. Even remembering how absolutely riveted I was as a teenager by another song, a wildly surreal musical eruption of insolence about the incomprehension between generations, between predecessors and successors, half a century later I found it almost completely losing its power when my own teenage successor heard it in the car and concluded it was as faintly ridiculous as the rest of his father's sixties pretensions. *"He screams back, 'You're a cow'*?" mocked Parker. "What the fuck?" As it happens, I last listened to "Blind Willie McTell" on September 10, 2001, noting how even the song's lines of horror and abomination were beautiful in the poetry of their expression and singing. Watching over and over film of the next day's attack with "Blind Willie McTell" playing in my mind, I've never been able to hear it again.

ROUND MIDNIGHT

TO: JESSE G. PRESLEY

APRIL 4, 1974

You lunatic,

What can we say to make you stop? The novelty of your appearance in our pages having worn off some years ago, your latest psychotic outburst (which we return herewith) well exhausts whatever once might have been considered amusing about your "aesthetic" posture. Surely by now any deranged following that your "work" attracted has moved on to more certifiable diversions. Moreover, were it common editorial practice to include 45 rpm singles as part of our review coverage, we likely would reserve such space and ink for releases that actually exist, which apparently—as established by inquiries to various recording companies and outlets—the subject of your new tirade does not. (Presumably this explains why you write nothing of the record's music itself and refuse to offer the artist's name.) No one, we might add, has heard of "Luna Recording." Please allow us to pretend that you don't exist either, and be advised that further missives in this vein may be turned over to the proper authorities. You have become a scary person.

Sincerely,

THE EDITORS

"O Souverain" / "Oh Shenandoah"
[recording artist's name withheld]
(Luna Recording)

Behold the Death Disc, ~~motherfuckers cocksuckers~~
~~little darlins ladies & gents boys & girls whoever y'all~~
motherfuckers, by which I don't mean just any disc but rather
this one with its two-sided siren-seductions most peculiar
and ruinous: because y'all know by now I am the God of the
Black Yawp & Unholy Squall come to stare this doom square
in its cyclopean central eye and set alight the fuse between
the rest of us and said disc's portal to hell. For years I've
been warning you and now the fuliginous evidence is here in
my grasp. In these final hours past midnight I scribble this
in haste before sleep overtakes my poor self, given as how
every slumber hurls me back atop a black tower in a time
and country when and where I was never born, and given as
how I never can be certain that every night that final leap
will be into the gust that blows me to this whole other life
altogether where I might almost believe I belong instead of
him. Where I might almost believe I'm not *the wrong one*. So
this is no mere critique. This is a manifesto, the last will and
declaration of Jesse G. de Presley that I hereby shall scour
this one nation under a groove to its most forsaken corners
in order to search out and destroy every last copy extant of
this damnable 45 recording. Who decided forty-five was the
correct number of revolutions anyway, I do hereby propound?
Why not sixty like the minutes or twenty-four like the hours?

Why not 1,776 or 2,001 like the birth & death dates on a
country's tombstone? Who accepted forty-five as the speed at
which we hear and fathom each other? Because I surely do
not, you ~~pussies cunts sodomites pighumpers cains & abels~~
~~ahuras & ahrimans iras & charlies phils & dons brians &~~
~~dennises rays & daves duanes & greggs williams & jims liams~~
~~& noels jesses & elvises~~ pussies, I hear everything at my own
chosen speed, that is to say O (zero). I hear what the Death
Disc sings when it's not even spinning on the platter-player.
~~Candy died for *this*, God damn it?~~ I surely am certain y'all
been highly amused these years, I'm altogether confident
you've had your laugh these years at my various and tedious
rube-hickeries that you peg me for. I spent a lifetime believing
no song could be worthy of my wrath, no song could be big
or intimate enough for my vengeance—that all songs are
bound for whatever rubble to which the rest of us are duly
destined, all the songs of Another Place and Time. But now I
come for Everyone & Everything, you hear? Now I scavenge
the shops and ravage the bins. I plunder the turntables for
every last trace of every last copy that will be cast on a pyre
or shattered in half, its sharpest, most jagged edge slitting the
throat of every last traitor who opens to this his filthy ears.
Every melody will run with ~~blood tears~~ blood to the Ocean of
Noise, what with my brain a-flamin' and burnin' a hole where
I lie and nothing to cool me so I might just turn to smoke. I
will purify the airwaves, be they playing at O rpm or 2,001 or
anything in between. See y'all at the fucking inferno.

JGP

NEW YORK POST

SUSPECT IN '68 MURDER
OF POL TIED TO ARSON

Washed-Up Warhol
deviant on the loose

NEW YORK CITY, May 12—A "person of interest" in the slaying six years ago of a former United States senator and presidential candidate has been linked by authorities to a string of downtown firebombings in recent weeks.

Following the April 8 blaze that destroyed a Greenwich Village music store at Macdougal and 3rd Streets, half a dozen fires have gutted other local outlets as well as the "Church," a legendary Columbia Records studio on 30th Street, whose April 19 inferno hit the industry hard.

Police refuse to name the suspect but according to sources ongoing investigation centers on Jesse G. Presley, age undetermined and of whom little else is known other than his involvement in the June 3, 1968, shooting of a onetime rising star in Democratic Party politics and Massachusetts scion of a former ambassador to the United Kingdom. The bizarre incident drew national attention and led to the closing of the notorious Factory, a Lower Manhattan "performance" and "art" venue on which premises the murder took place. (Subsequent inquiry suggested that Presley, who was not charged in the shooting, may have been the original target.)

Previous to two of the latest arson fires, a man matching the suspect's description was overheard having altercations characterized as "frightening" and "unhinged" with shopkeepers regarding the sale of an unfamiliar recording. Allegedly the suspect threatened one owner with retribution and in another instance angrily questioned the manager's veracity with a strange canine reference.

Authorities also have been alerted by the editorial offices of a locally published jazz journal to recent communication from the suspect of an ominous and unstable nature. On further questioning, editors of "Round Midnight" magazine acknowledge sporadically publishing writings by the suspect in past years but vehemently dispute assertions that they encouraged the criminal behavior under investigation.

Despite editors' claims the 45 rpm recording that may have triggered the arson spree in fact does not exist, the victimized merchants in question insist the suspect appeared to have a copy with him during their confrontations.

Police refuse to comment on speculation that Presley may no longer be in the greater New York area.

In possession of nothing but the clothes on his back and a 45 rpm record in a plain white sleeve, Jesse rides the night train from New York to DC and Richmond, Virginia, too, on to Raleigh and Atlanta, not forgetting New Orleans, home of the blues. He is part fugitive on the run and part man on a mission to kill American song and eradicate from the countryside the recording's every last copy, hunting down the studio and headquarters of Luna Recording so as to cut the song mute at its source. Jesse gets off in New Orleans just feet from the city's most fabled district, where he has heard that doorways ring in arpeggios, overhanging oaks weep harmonics, and trilling naked women welcome from their verandas the train's male passengers. Spying from his train no such uninhibited welcome, he finds the city under the pall of the same quietude that greets his every stop.

A mysterious silence overtakes the country. Jesse might as well ask where America is when he asks the French Quarter bartender how to find the neighborhood that was once meant to contain American freedom and frenzy with its American whores and horn players, American johns and sax tooters, American pimps and pianists, American drunks and drummers in the pastel-psychedelik of winding staircases and windows from which one might leap—as Jesse once did from a tower rooftop—into an American night of buried memories unearthed or unlived lives lived. Containing American song and whatever wild voice sings it, whatever wild possibility composes it, whatever wild heart loves it, because nothing is more deeply American than the deeply forbidden, the district was intended to quarantine that song and above all else keep everything outside the quarantine from getting too damned American. The bartender informs Jesse that the part of town he searches for has been gone sixty years. Taking no chances, convinced that lunacy if not music resides in the neighborhood where that hooker's self-mythologized son who claimed to be born on July 4, 1900, went on to invent the twentieth century by the age of crucifixion, in the final minutes before dawn and the next train out Jesse sets Iberville and Basin alight anyway, their flickers growing to flames behind him, the rising daybreak sun a drop of neon blood in the smoke.

impunity (train)

He knows that soon authorities will trace his trajectory of fire and follow. He heads toward a west that is the dreamer's true north, where the desert comes looking for us and curls at the door, a wild animal made of our ashes; hijacking the sun halfway, Jesse leaves his shadow at the crossroad. For the first time since his mad leap into his other life, he hears in his head the singing that is his voice but isn't. Among the train's passengers is talk of a shadow track that cuts through the heart of the century from one end to the other with impunity, as though no time exists of calibration or counting, only an era of the mind. Every shadow hides a shaft to the center of the Earth, from which blows the gust of cancellation. In the distance, like the train's whistle, out of the dream-strafed countryside beyond Jesse's window, the singing in his head grows louder the farther the train rounds Vegas's nuclear id, where the flesh of the world is tattooed with light. In the last days of summer, nine mornings before the fall, finally he stops a few miles from the sea, near the beginning of a highway that's one six short of the devil's sign.

Enthralled by doom and deliverance, and with a tunnel where his heart should be, from the station Jesse makes his way south through the wasteland of what he discerns almost immediately to be the strangest city of all time, a city hostile to its own being. A mile and a half away at Main and Sixth, he checks into the Hotel Desamor, its fifteen-floor brick side emblazoned with weekly rates. Pushing the hotel register to Jesse across the front desk, the clerk stares at him. "Is it you?" he asks.

"No," says Jesse.

"How would you know it's not you unless it *is* you?"

"Whoever you think it is," says Jesse, "I'm not."

The clerk says, "Haven't you been a guest at this hotel before?"

"No," says Jesse.

"Just a few weeks ago?"

"No."

"This is your first time?" the clerk says, unconvinced.

"Yes."

The clerk continues to stare at him. "Are you sure?"

"Yes, sir." Jesse signs the hotel register "E. Aron Shadowborne." He's in his room on the hotel's highest floor less than ten minutes when the telephone rings.

He doesn't answer the first time, but when it rings again, he picks it up. "Mr. Shadowborne?" asks the voice on the other end. "Yes," Jesse answers as noncommittally as anyone can when answering yes. The voice on the telephone says, "This is Mr. Axton. I'm the manager of the hotel. I just wanted to welcome you back."

"Yes, sir," answers Jesse. "Thank you. 'Back'?"

There's a pause. The manager says, "You were with us a few weeks ago, correct?"

"No, sir."

"Perhaps you've forgotten."

"No, sir. I've never been in this here hotel before, or this here city." Lying on the bed, Jesse can see the locks on the door from any place in his room; it's the sort of room in which one can see any place in it from any other place. Other than a single chair and a stool small enough to be useless, there are only a tiny TV on a high shelf and a drawing of the hotel in its inaugural year, 1927, when Charles Lindbergh flew the Atlantic and sound disturbed the movies. Jesse places the sleeved 45 before the screen of the TV. Travel brochures in the room promise that the Desamor is "minutes away" from everything, but the Desamor has never been minutes away from anything worth being minutes away from. Halls and mezzanine fill with strange languages; strange men wander the dim corridors counting their fingertips, lips moving silently. The sink and shower barely drip from the lack of water pressure.

lonely street

At night Jesse studies the door's bolt and two latches that were added when one of the hotel's guests was recently arrested for murdering fourteen women in the nearby hills. Another—a journalist on assignment from the East Coast—was apprehended for strangling three prostitutes. When someone knocks on the door at the Desamor, it's never room service, or not the kind that anyone orders. Over the years heartbroken lovers have leapt to their deaths from the Desamor's rooms; in the thirties a woman landed on a pedestrian strolling below, killing him. Even the sidewalks of the Desamor are dangerous. Other guests in the hotel stop and gawk at Jesse; someone matching his description disappeared three weeks ago, last seen dashing alone into the elevator. Jesse hears people muttering behind his back and imagines WANTED signs for him in every room but his. He steals a DO NOT DISTURB sign from a neighboring door and puts it outside his own. Later that evening he finds the sign hanging on another door down the hall—the floor's most coveted item, like lamb's blood on egyptian entries ushering Death on Its way. Staring at his ceiling in the dark, he listens to the screams of angels falling from heaven.

The roar of *find a new place to* rousing him from his non-sleep, he lurches upward one night from his bed to note the frayed curtains blowing before his wide-open window. He has no recollection of opening his window. With a start he sees what he takes to be himself—understanding, of course, that it's not—sitting at the foot of the bed. Maybe, he thinks, the other has come to steal back his 45 from off the shelf, but in the dark Jesse still makes out the white sleeve leaning against the small TV. The other one at the foot of his bed is soaking wet; in the gleam of city lights coming through the window, beads drip down his brother's face. "Why now, Jess," he says quietly, without mockery, even a bit sadly, "what do you suppose it is you done changed with all your commotion?" Rising from the bed he adds, "But you gettin' close now, big bro, so just follow me," stepping to the sill and out the window. "No!" Jesse calls, unsure later what he means by it. He waits to hear the thud of a body hitting the street, or the cry of someone on the walkway killed by a falling twin. When Jesse wakes the next morning, if it's waking, he's not surprised to find the foot of the bed damp, as he once found the carpet stained with her blood after "dreaming" of his mother.

He showers, brushes his teeth, and washes himself as best he can, given the lack of water pressure. When he hears a ruckus in the hall outside, he opens the door to the sight of police scurrying past him and up the side stair to the roof, where what remains of the guest who's been missing three weeks—and for whom everyone has mistaken Jesse—is found in the rooftop water tank. Jesse studies the drip of the faucet, the wet washcloth in his hands, the water glass by his bed. Leaving the Hotel Desamor, heading west on foot, he never quite stops glistening with the dead man, like someone covered with ash from a ritual.

With the sun at his back, Jesse sweats the dead man from inside him, the corpse's surviving twin making his way among the termini of the last American city, along roads named after flora and fountains and setting suns. Less than a mile from the Desamor, he passes a once grander, now deserted hotel where, from the eighth-floor balcony overlooking a square named for a World War I general, a once destined president bushwhacked by the zeitgeist regarded the city before him with all its high black windows, and music rained from a hole in the sky.

Notwithstanding the creak of pink sky-gondolas swaying high in the distance like blown petals of a dead rose, now the city is hushed and the sky rains nothing. Crossing the Spandrel of Murmurs at a far boulevard named for terraces of the moon, Jesse sings to keep himself company—a man who's bitten his tongue to kill any song at its tip, who never has sung but to prove to others and himself who he isn't. Day's end he reaches the foot of the Hollywood Hills in a section of town identified by the Desamor desk clerk as Bloozpark.

Exhausted and famished, in pursuit of Luna Recording and clutching the 45 in its white sleeve that's falling apart, Jesse finds a spot under one of the crumbling footbridges sweeping small pools of black lava that bubble up from the cracked earth. When he wakes, he's nestled in a wooden cage suspended off a dirt cliff. He sees a city whose spires are the rotted masts of landlocked boats, tattered sails bearing meaningless insignia. Lanterns flare from charred ports and starboards and the silhouettes of moldering prows jutting from the hillsides. On overgrown sidewalk corners, deserted intersections are marked by antique telescopes stuck skyward.

Past the ridge a quarter mile away, noise ascends and falls, glass breaks, men and women cry out. From the beached boats rises the occasional old hotel built by now-dead film studios, guns in its windows glinting from the plunge of a senseless sun. Half its neon letters burned out, US O & FR N reads the sign of a shuttered restaurant. Jesse can hear animals stampeding in the canyon. Damned if he has the slightest idea where he is; in his first few moments of waking, he remembers dreaming—or what he believes may have been dreaming, in his usual sleeping state that's too fitful for sleep—of being lifted and carried.

As he gazes below in the twilight, his is the only white face in the midst of gathering black faces, as many as several hundred. Some are in a clearing close by small fires, others are perched in their windows and leaning against half-earthed hulls. Some watch their prisoner with only mild curiosity and others ignore him. All around, Jesse hears a bottleneck of music from every avenue, jams and solos, grooves and refrains. He realizes that, other than the tune in his head and on his own lips earlier this day—or was it yesterday?—and other than the torched record shops and studios in his wake that went up in lullabies of smoke, it's the first music he's heard since he can remember, or maybe since what he can't remember.

twilight song

From his suspended cage, Jesse can see to the west a valley pass threaded by a vacated freeway. In the foothills to the east is the mouth of a large tunnel, and carved out of the hillside beside his cage is a small cove where a guard is posted. An open trumpet case sits beside the guard, horn undisturbed. In the arm's reach that separates Jesse from his sentry is a drop of twenty feet. "Say there, son," calls Jesse.

"I am not," answers the guard, "your son, *son.*"

"I surely would appreciate knowing how long I can expect to sit up in this here sky."

"Until he comes," answers the guard, but no one arrives that evening or the next morning when Jesse wakes to a voice that, even at a speed too slow, he recognizes as his but not. This time it isn't in his head but rather broadcasts from a small round piece of vinyl revolving somewhere on a child's old turntable. *Oh Shenandoah, I long to hear you*, great national metamorphosis song; and only then does Jesse belatedly understand he no longer has with him the 45. Noon passes and then afternoon. It's almost twilight again when people below suddenly are in motion, a lone figure on foot appearing in the mouth of the eastern tunnel that runs underground from Jefferson Boulevard eight miles south. The tall, almost professorial man walks out of the firelight as Jesse's cage is lowered into the hubbub.

Malik

Loping purposefully, distinguished and wearing dark-rimmed glasses, he is well over six feet and nearing fifty years. His black face and beard are tinged red, as though permanently reflecting all the fires passed in his life, his hair the coppery hue genetically passed down from the white maternal grandfather who raped his black grandmother. Everyone parts for his entrance and closes behind him as he reaches the open space to study Jesse's captivity.

"Behold," he says finally and turns to the others, "the cracker. By which I do not mean just any cracker but a cracker truly cracked in two, the first of him having swallowed the second, the steam of his missing half rising from his flesh. On the one hand we might call him . . . liberator," he chuckles, the surrounding crowd chuckling with him if not sure at exactly what, "since he has displaced his other half and thereby liberated us from the white-trash devil who stole our music, stole our style, stole the sound from our ears and the song from our mouths, so as to purvey them to twenty million white adolescent females in the menstrual throes of their black-man fantasies. The so-called King is dead. Long rot the king."

"On the other hand, brothers and sisters," he says, calmly raising a single finger pointed at Jesse, "on the other hand we might call him oppressor, having displaced his other half, who, as nothing less but nothing more than a guileless white fool, opened the white door through which rushed black consciousness, infiltrating the white experience. The other half who, in his limited way, educated white-devil America that it was 'colored folk,' as he put it so quaintly—colored folk 'that nobody paid no mind'—who sang and played the music of the so-called Negro shanties and juke joints for years before his white ass knew what it was. 'I got it from them,' as he put it so directly once, giving credit where it was due."

A young woman brings a cup to the tall professor, who disdainfully regards what's in it before pouring it on the ground. The young woman appears crestfallen, mumbling apologies—"Never mind," he says, "just get me water"—and Jesse realizes that for the first time since he arrived in Bloozpark, all the music and bar noise has succumbed to the rest of the country's silence, but for the speaker. "Now, when I was in prison," he says, taking a cup of water from another young woman, "I became a man of words. Mr. Dreiser. Herr von Goethe. The Viscount Morley," he says, "of Blackburn. White men, let it be acknowledged and noted—not Negro professors with their PhDs in Advanced Uncle Tomism— white men who, in brief epiphanies, overcame their inner devils to grasp truth. In prison I pondered words and their meanings. So for a moment, brothers and sisters, let us ponder together the meaning of the word *strain*, and as we do, let us ponder our dilemma long enough to realize it is no dilemma at all, because whether the cracker is cracked one way or the other, oppressor or liberator, our resolve does not change, our strategy is cracked too, but cracked in a manner less fractured than wise and multipurposed. We shall trust whatever part of the cracker's misbegotten life we can make of value to us, the only value his life ever had until this moment from the moment he was born, that value being his life's capacity for white destruction. We shall be wary as well, because he is a white fool in whose being, as in the being of any white fool, lies our destruction, too. No other recourse makes sense than that we be both wary and trustful at once. To do only one is to miss the opportunities or warnings of the other. In the meantime, as for the word *strain*," he concludes with a small smile, "it has numerous meanings. Of course, *strain* can mean an effort that involves great exertion. It can mean something stretched to a fragile if not ultimately broken point. But most irresistibly for our purposes, most fascinating is that somehow, for some unfathomably philologic reason, the same word that applies to a virus also is used to describe a theme of music."

get ready

Tossing and turning in his cage once again, that night Jesse dozes to the distant crackling—through one of the nearby windows—of the 45 played over and over. Although the unfamiliar flipside of "Oh Shenandoah" is sung in a foreign language, in semi-consciousness Jesse hears the lyric in English anyway, in what is or is not his voice, more spoken than sung.

Here come the planes, so you better . . .

When he finally shakes himself to consciousness with a start, unmistakably the cage is settled on solid ground, with its door open.

The night around him beginning to pale in the east, Jesse pulls himself out.

No one else is in sight. He follows the sound of the 45 across a square, passing embers of fires blazing hours before, along stone steps winding up the foothills to a house in the trees enshrouded in leaf and shrub. Berserk scents of ebb tide blow in with the squawk of distant gulls. At the top of the steps, a small wooden patio leads into a long single room where the record plays, although it takes Jesse a moment in the dark to determine the alcove with the turntable.

He stands over the turntable watching its arm and stylus reach the end of the record, then rise from the final groove and return to the beginning. For a while Jesse is transfixed by the notion of a song playing endlessly, when his eyes drift in the dark to other records filed next to the turntable, a poster on the alcove wall for "jazz at Massey Hall" by "the quintet," as though there could be only one quintet that mattered, which in this case is nearly so. Finally Jesse realizes that the tall professorial man who addressed him and the gathered townspeople hours earlier is lying on a mattress just feet away.

While the man appears asleep, Jesse makes out the glint of dawn off the dark-rimmed glasses on his face. Jesse takes the needle from the record and takes the record from the turntable; the plain white sleeve that's held the 45 all this time is nowhere to be seen. Suddenly Jesse is seized by a certainty. "Luna," he says out loud, convinced he's found what he's looking for, although if he thought about it at all he would realize this doesn't make sense. The sleeper along the wall stirs. "Only loon in this room, my man," Jesse hears from the mattress, "is you."

Jesse says, "Figured you was awake. The glasses."

"Even in my darkness," comes the reply, "I remain a man of vision. I would have smelled the devil from you in any case, the moment you entered my room—that steam of your missing half and the cloud of malignancy about you."

"Yes, sir," agrees Jesse.

"Of course I do not approve of music. The only music Allah listens to is the desert wind blowing from Mecca. Notwithstanding the righteous aspirations of Brothers Monk and Trane, bop is the sound of my corrupted past exhaling its dying breath, the jungle sigh of lindy-hopping and reefers and burning lye in the hair to make it white-devil straight. The sobs of women I pimped, passing as ecstatic moans in the way a fallen brother attempts to pass for white. In prison, I renounced music for words. But just between us, the world's angriest black man and a white-devil intruder in the dark—"

"Well now, about that, this *is* my record and you *did* take it, after all. . . ."

"—just between the two of us, I cannot resist a taste now and then, like the reformed drunk who has to have a nip of whisky now and then, like the confessed fornicator who cannot resist now and then a strange woman's comfort. I cannot resist just the smallest taste of Bird or Her Majesty the Queen, Miss Dinah Washington. 'Teach Me Tonight.' 'Blue Gardenia.' 'Big Long Slidin' Thing' . . . just"—Jesse hears him laugh low in the dark— "a little taste."

"Well," says Jesse, "you must like this record to play it over and over."

"No. No." Something about the other man's voice changes. "No. I just . . . it has a secret," he says, "it has a shadow."

"You think you're going to figure that out by playing it over and over?"

"No. I play it every time hoping the secret remains unrevealed. I play it every time for the relief at the end, the relief of glimpsing and feeling as little of the shadow as I did at the beginning."

"Sir," says Jesse solemnly, "I have come to kill American song."

"Yes," answers the voice in the dark, "what you're looking for is down among the eucalyptuses. You'll know it when you see it."

Beyond the eucalyptuses, on the shredded remnants of a mast's sail, the insignia is faded beyond recognition to anyone who doesn't know it as well as Jesse: the worn image of him side by side with his brother, each with six-gun drawn from a holster as though in a Western gunfight. No cowboy hat, long-sleeve buttoned shirt, and boots and jeans double-belted with holster slung low on the right hip; together the twins look not square into the camera but ever so slightly off. The door of the boat's cabin, beneath the sail's slightly fluttering tatters, is open and black.

Striding through, Jesse descends the ship's spiraling steps and continues far deeper than he would have thought a boat's hull could go, his confusion only compounded when he reaches the bottom and a door with light behind it. He pushes the door open, trying to determine what surprises him more than the light—the old man, or the wraparound window behind his desk, through which can be seen the unrolling of a bustling city boulevard and a college in the distance, the lattice of winter-woven trees before an Atlantic that surely seems the wrong ocean altogether.

The old man glances up. "Oh," he says, nodding at Jesse. "For a moment," he explains, "I thought you were One Nation Under—"

"I'm Jesse," says Jesse.

"I see now."

"This is Luna Recordings?"

"Recording."

"What? Sir," Jesse says with no small impatience, "I should tell you I've been scorching my way across this here nation in order to find Luna Recordings."

The old man appears exhausted. He is unshaven and what he still has of his hair has gone white. "Well," he says, "here you are."

Jesse says, "I should warn you that I mean no good whatsoever, searching out and destroying every one of these hellacious hunks of tarnation I can find"—he holds up the naked 45 in his hand—"or everywhere that might carry such a one on its premises or in its possession. And I don't mean to stop now."

Jesse gazes at the chamber around him. The furniture is topsy-turvy, an armoire pushed to where it doesn't belong. "If this is Luna Recordings," he asks, "where are all the recordings?"

"Recording."

"What?"

"I'm not trying to annoy you," the old man says, "but I believe if you look at the label, it says, 'Recording.' Singular."

"Singular?" Jesse looks at the 45. Picking his way through his thoughts, he finally says, "You trying to tell me that Luna Recordings, or Recording, has made only one record?"

"It would seem."

"Well then," Jesse shakes his head, "where are the other copies?"

The old man nods at the 45 in Jesse's hand. "Like I said. Singular."

Jesse stares hard at the world's most obscure author and says, as evenly as he can manage, "Are you telling me that the whole of Luna Recording is one single copy of one single record?" He gazes around him again, eyes hovering for a while on the bustling lights outside the window. Slowly he reaches down for one of the overturned chairs on the floor and sets it upright, sitting. For what seems a longer time than it is, the two don't converse again, until Jesse finally says quietly, "I do believe that this here life has made a damn fool of me."

"I know," the old man says as quietly. "Me too."

"I was the wrong one."

"I'm sorry."

Jesse tosses to the side the 45 that has brought him thousands of hours and miles. "Well, I wonder what now, sir."

From his own chair, the author unbends himself. "Let me show you," he says.

paternity

Parker and Zema were not in their father's life long before he knew he wouldn't want to be in any life without them. The moment of dying is banal unless you've been dying long enough to watch death approach and give it meaning; the moment of loss is banal unless you've been losing long enough to feel what slips away and to calibrate its retreat. Whether or not Parker and Zema's father might be old enough to say he lived with death daily, he long grasped, psychologically if not emotionally, existence's precariousness.

When he was his daughter's age—the age that she is now as she crosses the country in their father's Camry with her brother—a friend of his mother's took a shower one morning and discovered a lump on her back just below her neck. Six weeks later, the woman was dead, departed with such dizzying hurry that Parker and Zema's father never forgot it. Although it might be that he's just one for drama, he honestly can claim that rarely a day goes by when he isn't conscious of the possibility it's his last.

The year before his son's birth, Parker's father was in an auto accident outside Chicago. His car hit the rain on the highway in such a way as to send the vehicle spinning across three lanes of rush-hour traffic while inexplicably avoiding collision, then off the highway down a knoll and across a field into a wood, rather than caroming off a concrete wall back into all the traffic he had just narrowly missed. Drama or no, he could justifiably go so far as to later call his survival of the incident freakish, comparable to scenes in a Western when a perfectly placed tin star stops a bullet from entering the marshal's heart.

The father isn't so stupid or dishonest as to say death doesn't frighten him. Death terrifies him. The oblivion of it, the finality that would make some part of a person want to know when he wakes that morning—even as the rest of him denies it—that this is to be his final day. On a warm winter's morning two decades after that near-miss outside Chicago, he picks up a prescription for his migraines, drops Parker off at the local community college, begins preparing for the seminar he is scheduled to teach two days later, and with Zema in the car goes down the hill for the single purpose of getting some cash at an automated teller so that, the next day, he can pay the gardener who comes twice a month.

Not counting the auto accident, Zema's father has died at least once before, in Berlin at the turn of the century. That was a literary death, however, and no matter how much literature insists otherwise, it's not the same; literary deaths don't do banal, or know from the sad poetry that is banality. Because Zema is eleven years old on this day, her father finally lets her sit in the front seat as she's been demanding to since she was six. The breeze that brushes his face when he turns from the ATM to see the three men is lovely, and from the window of his car comes "Don't Explain," which isn't at all about this moment or the mysteries of how life begins and ends. *I'm glad you're bad*, the singer sings to her faithless lover, *don't explain*.

Zema's father pivots too sharply to the car once he realizes what's happening. "Dad?" Zema calls from the front seat. One of the young men turns to look too. When he sees the girl he says, "That your daughter? That's not your daughter." The father calls back to her, "Don't look," then to the men, "She hasn't seen your faces," and the girl lunges from the passenger seat to the other side of the car. She bolts from the driver's door into oncoming traffic— a flight that, preposterously, she'll feel guilty about forever. The horrified father cries out, lurching to her; slammed back against the ATM by the three men, he takes his hands from his face to look.

the song that may or may not be true

Miraculously, Zema stands in the boulevard's center divider, gazing back. In the cascade of second, third, fourth thoughts, she takes a step toward her father before he says, "Go," more calmly than he would think possible, at a volume that no one would think she could hear over traffic; and she goes. At that moment, more than anything, more than despondency or torment, he feels the sweet sorrow of having loved his little girl and knowing that this is the last time he'll see her, of feeling the magnitude of missing her that is an eternity's worth of feeling. She dashes across the rest of the boulevard and keeps going until she's run out of his life into some new perdition of her own imagining that no one else could possibly believe she deserves. *Where*, she will ask herself years later on the steps of a church in Valentine, *was a woman sheriff with a gray ponytail when we needed her?*

Those years later, on the last miles out of Nebraska, before falling asleep at the wheel just long enough to wake on a secret highway running through the country, her brother will be overwhelmed by his sister's sorrow, finally trying to tell her, to no avail, "It's not your fault." He will hear from her a whisper that mourns the lost family she never knew and the found family to which she never could quite convince herself she belongs, that mourns the lost code of identity and the secret message of the self that are neither deciphered nor disclosed. "White," the eleven-year-old Zema answers the police, hours after the ATM and back home at the dining room table where her father used to rail about stereo and MP3s, her stricken mother across the table from her, Parker ashen and furiously mute. The black female officer looks at Zema gently, waiting just long enough before pressing. "Are you sure, honey?" she says. "It was dark. We . . . have security footage, you know. Cameras that film it all. So maybe," a bit more assertively, "you're mistaken. Maybe," she adds, "it's what you think your father would want you to say"—at which point the hue of Zema's flesh, of which she became conscious the moment she became conscious of her new country, is rendered one more mystery of her life.

The first song because any national discography
that excludes it invalidates itself, and the second because
when the singer sings, *As I walk this land of broken
dreams*, it becomes clear that the thing breaking his
heart is the very land itself that he walks.

tracks 24 and 25:
"Oh Shenandoah" and "O Souverain"

Both songs are recorded by the most famous singer who ever lived on the night of either February 23 or February 25, 1971—although it's not clear if both are on the same night or over the two nights—near the end of the singer's third engagement at Las Vegas's then-named International Hotel, later the Las Vegas Hilton. No physical recording, as far as is known, exists on vinyl, disc, or tape, the performances only surfacing on YouTube without visual accompaniment but for a still photo that may or may not have been taken before the performances disappeared into thin air as ruthlessly and mysteriously as they appeared. There is no accompaniment other than the singer playing piano, and speculation has it, based on the regrettable sound quality, which suggests a rudimentary tape recorder and too much plush carpeting, that this rendition of the songs occurs in suite 3000, his hotel penthouse. Given the singer's release the following year of a track called "An American Trilogy"—a mash-up of spirituals and national folk tunes including "Dixie," "The Battle Hymn of the Republic," and "All My Trials"—it's somewhat surprising that the singer never committed to more professional documentation

"Oh Shenandoah," the great national metamorphosis song, originally a musical bulletin from the American future sent back to the nineteenth century from across the wide Missouri River, a hundred songs in one depending on who sang it or when it was heard over the past two hundred years: pioneer song, sailing song, slave song, Confederate song, French trader's love song for his

Indian bride. The flip side, "O Souverain," is as startling as "Oh Shenandoah" seems obvious and arguably the single strangest recording made by the singer, even acknowledging formidable competition from the likes of "Yoga Is as Yoga Does," a 1967 duet with a sixty-five-year-old British actress best known for playing the Bride of Frankenstein three decades earlier, and 1968's "Dominic the Impotent Bull" (*Moo, moo, move your little foot, do*) from a forgotten movie called *Stay Away, Joe*. As far as is authenticated by any historical log or record, no indication exists in the form of personal or written testimony or any witness's account that the singer would in any way be familiar with a fin-de-siècle French aria that's part prayer and part plea, even as an excursion into the European quasi-classical isn't unprecedented; upon his discharge from the army a decade before, he turned a Naples serenade into what was, at the time and under a different title, his biggest hit yet and reportedly his favorite recording, and then turned another classical piece written before the French Revolution into an even bigger hit, also under a different title. The Neapolitan "O sole mio," however, not only was already familiar to American audiences [*It's now or never*, sings the presidential candidate to himself, having heard it on his balcony falling like rain from a missing piece of the sky] but already was Americanized in an earlier version by another singer at the end of the forties, while the French "Plaisir d'amour" has a hymnlike melody to which one can't help falling in love, so haunting as to have inspired through the centuries composers and authors from Berlioz to Hesse. "O Souverain," on the other hand—a musical bulletin from the American future sent back to the twentieth century—won't attain currency with American music fans in any configuration until another decade later and after the singer's death, and then not by way of the singer's rendering, unknown for still another thirty years, but rather the interpretation of a female performance artist from the Midwest who translates and assimilates the aria into a larger eight-minute surrealist soundscape that itself is part of an eight-hour opus titled *United States*. Twenty years after its release and thirty years after this subterranean recording by the singer so famous that it seems nothing in his life or music could still have been subterranean, the same performance artist from the Midwest performs the song in the same city where she recorded it, just days and miles from the obliteration of that city's World Trade Center, to audible gasps from the audience when she sings the lines, *Here come the planes, so you better get ready*. Is the most famous singer who ever lived gripped by a prophecy he doesn't know, voicing this aria that he has no reason to know—or does he decide, as well he might, that the true prophecy remains "Oh Shenandoah" (*Roll away, you rolling river*), a conclusion reached by the singer only upon finishing the song, closing his eyes, closing the keyboard on the piano, exiting the suite, making his way in his private elevator down to the Vegas Strip, stepping into the limousine waiting for him, and, from the backseat, hearing the sound of a train in the distance. Turning to the window and for a moment forgetting that his other half is nothing but a fetal shell once curled in an old shoe box on a kitchen table beside the bed where his mother gave birth to her sons, and for a moment forgetting all the times over the years that he has visited the small, unmarked grave back in Tupelo's Priceville Cemetery where he would wonder how it is that he's the one who made it instead, he whispers "Jesse?" so inaudibly that he cannot even be certain whether he hopes his brother answers.

Now Jesse hears his own name whispered in his ear, whispered as close as if his brother is standing there next to him. He turns to gaze around at the flat silvery mesa over which shines an enormous ashen orb that he can't be sure is an eclipsed sun or a full moon bursting the far horizon of the brightest night. The old man from Luna Recording is nowhere to be seen, nor is the buried boat with the tattered double-trouble sail. All that Jesse confronts are the two massive open graves, transported from national recollection by the moan of three thousand ghosts; gazing back at the city in the distance, he has a feeling he's not in L.A. anymore, to coin a phrase, assuming he ever was in any L.A. that anyone has ever known as L.A. Damned, of course, if he has the slightest idea where he is, but he's gotten rather used to that by now, and isn't even certain that he sees anymore the point of knowing. But standing there small before the two enormous scorched cavities under the rumbling sky and under the mammoth moon the color of cinder, Jesse feels the bottom of himself drop out, feels his soul fall to his feet and keep going: He is a man disappearing not only from his life but from the cosmic annals of being. Softly he whispers back to no one around him, no more loudly than was his brother's whisper a moment ago, "I do believe that I am the loneliest man who ever lived, in the loneliest country there ever was." Staring into the distance at all the smoke billowing from all the fires that he's set behind him, he asks, "What have I done?" But no one is there to answer that either.

Here come the planes, so you better . . . Lying in bed on his last night in the last room of the Sonark that he's pillaged searching for his missing song, Parker and Zema's father no longer is certain if the lyric is something he actually hears or can just no longer get out of his head, like a virus. Things don't just disappear into thin air, but now the only thing of his that's left to vanish is whatever is left of himself; in the dark, thinking of his family, he feels his eyes leak down his face. He raises to his face his hands. Growing old, he's come to realize, is like traveling the round world for a long time—that you understand, in the end, isn't that long at all—until the shores of childhood drift into sight again, one's mind slipping the gears of time and accompanied only by the echoes of a song as everything else lurches into soundlessness. *Here ome th planes, so ou better* and now even that disappears too, a sound at a time. *Here ome th pl nes, so etter* and we're only our own Xs marking the spot on the map of ourselves. "Good-bye," he whispers in the dark to his wife and son and daughter, before it's too late, "g odby . I love y

air. Then as before, behind the wheel Parker hears him-self again . . . *wake up* . . . re-alizing then that—has it been only moments, or hours or days or years?—he has been if not asleep then somehow not present: he turns to confirm that his sister, Zema, still is in the passenger seat next to him, aware that, as there have been no exits on the Shadow-bahn that hurtles them onward through the shadowcountry and through the shadowcen-tury, as well there has been the most complete silence that he can remember hearing, not so much a hush vortex, because even a hush has a presence, but something that is outside sonics: and then suddenly the secret highway is gone altogether. Zema stirs and wakes. They're back on two-lane road pushing on into the Dakota night. Zema's music flickers on and off the closer they finally near the Badlands. As she sputters static, he peers over at her from the driver's seat until she snaps, "Why do you keep looking at me?"

He answers, turning back to the road, "Just making sure you're okay."

"Why wouldn't I be okay?"

He pauses. "Your music . . ."

"I know," she murmurs.

". . . keeps cutting out."

"I'm okay."

"I mean, it's not like some kind of vital sign or something?"

"No."

"Like the monitor that flatlines when it's hooked up to a hospital patient—"

"I don't know what the music thing's about."

"—or like your heart is skipping beats or anything."

"I'm fine."

"I just," he says, staring straight ahead at the highway, "want to be sure," and she looks at him, because although he's stated it in as much of a monotone and with as little affect as he can muster, never remotely has Parker said anything like it to her. "Probably should watch the road," is all she can think to answer.

Somewhere in the dark, Parker realizes he's on the wrong road. "This isn't the highway I thought we were on," he says to the pitch black before him, intermittently shredded by his headlights.

"Should we go back?" asks Zema.

"We're still going the right direction," he claims, "just . . . the wrong way in the right direction."

"Dad always said you have Mom's sense of direction. That means we could be going anywhere."

"I don't know where we would go back to."

"It feels like we're in the middle of—"

"You've been asleep, how would you know what it feels like?" In the distance are taillights. "There's someone." The taillights grow closer, and when Parker and Zema's Camry catches up, it's clear that the truck—red with gold racing stripes and, in Parker's headlights, a bumper sticker that reads SAVE AMERICA FROM ITSELF—has run off the side of the road. Zema sits up. "Is that person okay?"

"I don't want to stop," says Parker, continuing on.

"We ought to," she argues halfheartedly.

Stopping in the middle of the small highway, Parker turns in his seat and looks back at the truck's lights in the pitch black. "Do you think he's okay?" he asks.

"We shouldn't stop in the middle of the road," she answers, "someone could hit us."

"You just told me to stop. There's no one else out here."

"*That* person is out here."

"Fuck, all right," Parker says somewhat angrily.

"Don't make this like it's my idea."

"It *is* your idea," he says, circling the Camry around. Returning to the truck, the brother and sister pull up alongside it. The lights of the truck's cabin are on and its driver glances around in apparent confusion. "See, he's okay," says Parker, and Zema doesn't answer. Parker sighs and gets out, leaves the Camry running. He stops a few feet from the truck. The truck's driver sees him and rolls down his window and for a moment the two men just look at each other. "Are you okay?" Parker finally asks.

"I fell asleep at the wheel," comes from the truck. "Only for a second, but . . ." He pushes open the door and tries to dislodge himself from his front seat.

Parker moves as if to catch him but doesn't. "You need help?"

Aaron tumbles groggily to the ground. "I don't know," he says, but reaches out and Parker pulls him up. Aaron leans against the truck, holding his head. "I think I'm okay," he concludes without conviction.

Parker studies him. "Do you have a phone? Want to call someone?"

"Cell phones don't work out here, at least mine doesn't. Now and then I can get something on the radio. Of course there hasn't been any music lately—I don't have a disc player, but I guess even they don't play anything anymore." Aaron says, "A song finishes, I have no idea what I just heard. But at least it keeps me awake."

"Do you know if this is Interstate 90? I have a feeling we took a wrong turn."

"This is Highway 44. It goes where 90 goes."

"Can you drive?"

"I don't know. But I don't know if I can just leave my truck here, either." Trying to move, Aaron seizes his ribs; catching his breath, he says, "Well, I think I cracked something."

Parker looks back at Zema and the Camry, exhales deeply. "We can try to take you somewhere, if you need," he says. "You want to lock it up?"

Wincing, Aaron slowly surveys the truck's cabin. "Don't see my keys."

"They're not in the ignition?"

"No."

Parker goes around to the passenger's side of the truck and opens the door. "Well," he finally says, "they didn't just disappear into thin air."

The other man stares at him, suddenly more alert than he's been since Parker met him. "You still believe that?"

Aaron has been in the backseat of the Camry for ten minutes when he says, "You hear that?"

Parker and Zema in the front don't answer. In the rearview mirror, Parker can see Aaron painfully readjust himself upright, holding his side and listening; traffic is starting to pick up on the small highway, all of it coming from the other direction. "All the cars are coming from where we're going," says Zema.

"Do you hear that?" their passenger repeats. "It's . . ."

"Music," she says.

"Just bits, snatches . . . so you *do* hear it," and when neither the brother nor sister responds, Parker can see in the rearview mirror the realization come over Aaron's face. "You're her," says Aaron, "you're them. Supersonik."

"It cuts in and out," says Parker.

"All the traffic is in the other direction," says Zema again, watching the cars pass.

"It's not like a vital sign or anything," Parker explains to Aaron, "it's not like an irregular heartbeat. She's okay."

Aaron looks from one to the other. "So you're . . ."

"Brother and sister," says the sister.

"Absolutely," promises the brother.

"They're leaving," Aaron says to the window, nodding at the cars. "There's nothing there anymore, if that's where you're going."

"The Towers aren't there anymore?" says Zema.

"I was the first one," says Aaron.

"You were the first one what?"

"First to see them," he says as matter-of-factly as he can. "I'm not just saying it. It was on the news."

"You were first to see the Towers?"

"I'm not saying it was anything special about me. I just happened to be there when they appeared. If I hadn't got into an argument with Cilla Ann back on the other side of the Missouri—I can't even remember what about—I would have driven by the spot five minutes earlier, when they weren't there."

"How do you know they weren't there?" says Zema.

"How do we know they haven't been there the whole time?" says Parker.

Zema and Aaron both look at him. For a while the car is quiet. "Just saying," Aaron finally offers, "that I don't know how it is those Towers first showed up when I came along. That's all. But sometimes, honest to God, I . . . think none of it would have happened if I hadn't seen them to begin with." He adds, "I know how that sounds."

"Maybe," Parker suggests wryly, "the Towers saw your bumper sticker."

"I've never been able to figure out what that bumper sticker means. So," Aaron asks Zema, "do you think of a particular song and that's what comes out of you? Or is it more random? Does a song ever come out that you've never heard before?"

"I'm not a jukebox," she says.

Abandonment hemorrhages. Its moment turns into too many other moments at one time to be any river of such moments other than a flood: The collective bearing of witness collapses under the weight of its own hope and terror. Somewhere along the dark little highway the exodus turns mass, a long line of fleeing campers and trailers past which flies Parker and Zema's Camry going the other way.

"Stop," says Zema at almost the very place where Aaron stopped nine days before. In the distance the horizon's rim of night sky east of the Badlands glints dark blue before shimmering to silver, preluding a streak of the sun at dawn. As Parker stops, his sister gets out; after a moment the men get out with her. She stares northward agape. Aaron looks at her, looks at the empty northbound landscape, back at her. Parker just watches his sister, shaking his head and snorting with a perfunctory derision, but he can't help a small smile. "You see them, don't you?" he says.

"You see them?" says Aaron.

She turns to both of them. "You don't?" But she knows the answer, and pivots back to the two massive Towers before her.

As everyone who's come to the Towers has learned, they're never as close as they appear. Halfway between them and the Camry behind her, crossing the weathered rock, Zema stops to look back; she barely can make out her brother and Aaron, who's still holding his ribs and trying to see if his cell works as it did the first afternoon he stopped his truck in the middle of the road and called his wife. Now the sun is up and becoming warm enough that she pushes on, if for no other reason than to slip into the peak of the South Tower's shadow.

When she reaches its shade ten minutes later, the Tower blocks enough of the sun that, at this hour from this position on the landscape, able to see it in greater detail than before, nonetheless she finds herself tricked by the light anyway—or so she believes. She turns back to look behind her the same way that Sheriff Rae Jardin turned to look behind her the afternoon she entered the South Tower, raising one hand to her eyes in order to squint hard in the sun, except that where the sheriff saw tens or hundreds of thousands of people, Zema sees only the Camry and her brother, barely visible, alone, with whatever few stragglers were there now gone. Glancing back at the Tower's base, she still spies what she dismissed from her mind only moments before.

A few minutes closer to the building, there's no mistaking that at its base, in one of its many massive doors, stands a man, and the closer that Zema comes, the more clearly she recognizes him as not just any man. Five minutes closer, she stops again and looks. "It's you?" she calls. His hair is beginning to gray a bit now and his face is becoming lined, but she still recognizes him from all the posters that, as her brother loves to taunt her, she had on her walls when she was younger.

"No, darlin'," Jesse answers, too quiet for her to hear, "it's not." He hasn't any more idea how he got back here to the Tower than how he left that night when he disappeared from the rooftop; when he gazes up to the roof, it's too high to see without falling over.

"I didn't hear you," she calls, cupping her mouth with her hands.

"I said," cupping his own hands, "that I'm not him."

She's still walking. Half a minute later, close enough to speak without shouting, she says, "You look like him," *except older*, she almost adds but doesn't.

A look of anguish like she hasn't seen before sweeps his face. He opens his arms. "Can't sing me a lick." He laughs the saddest laugh. "I've tried, but . . ." He asks, "Now, how is it I can swear I hear him right this very minute? Is that just his voice in my head again, or you got yourself a radio? Or one of them newfangled music—"

"It's me."

"You?"

"It comes out of me."

"How's that?"

"I can't even hear me anymore." She asks, "What am I playing right now anyway?"

"One for the money, two for the show."

After a pause, she says in something of an outburst, "There's music coming out of me that's not mine."

He nods. "There's singing in my head that's not me." He peers beyond her. "Everybody up and left, looks like. T'was some kind of damn multitude once, as near as I recall."

She explains, "They don't think you're here anymore," by which she means the buildings, gesturing at them.

He looks behind him at the Towers. "Did they ever think I was here?"

"They don't think anything is here. I'm the only one." She says to the darkening sky, "It actually looks like it's going to rain. Should we go inside?"

"Well, darlin', not like the buildings rightly belong to me, so I guess you can do as you want."

Zema offers, "You can come with us. My brother's back there waiting."

"Don't know as I rightly belong anywhere else, I've come to suspect," answers Jesse, "so I believe maybe I shall just set myself down here to stay. Wouldn't mind someone to talk to, though, if you got a minute to spare. I mean, someone who knows I'm the wrong one but doesn't mind so much. Can't say I expected *anyone* to wander my way at this point, let alone a little colored girl—" and then, aghast, contrition mixing with the anguish, he pleads, "Say, I'm sorry there."

"It's all right," she says.

"Swear I didn't mean nothing by it."

"I know."

"Don't mind me, miss. I'm just a damn hillbilly."

"Okay. Just don't call me 'miss.'"

the song that starts all over again

After the tow truck picks up Aaron, Parker walks the direction where he saw his sister go, about as far as he thought his sister went when he last saw her. As she did, he stops to look back at their car, then turns back to scan the empty landscape before him, vacant of any sign of structure or human being. He almost calls her name but doesn't; he might ordinarily be concerned but isn't. He knows she'll be back, but not when. Back at the Camry, he turns on the air conditioner and has been sitting in the front seat a few minutes, still watching out the windshield, when music suddenly comes on the radio station.

He wasn't aware that the radio was on. It's the first music from the radio since Texas, or maybe he means New Mexico. The motel where he almost got into the fight with the Native American woman, that was in . . . he doesn't remember, maybe it was before New Mexico. Was there music then? He doesn't remember that either. But now the radio plays music, a tune he doesn't know, and as he waits for Zema he changes the station, and changes it again, and—music on all the stations now—keeps changing it, certain that, sooner or later, he'll find one of his father's favorite songs.

An inadequate acknowledgment

The egomaniacal author, whose antisocial tendencies are part of what made him a writer to begin with, likes to pretend he goes about his calling alone, some paladin of words wandering plains of blank pages without a Sancho Panza to his name, until he writes a novel such as this. Then the whole enterprise of the book—which is to say not just the conception and writing but what comes afterward—can be more tortured than for any other he's authored, for reasons and in ways that can be told later or by others. There are people for whom acknowledgment is barely enough, and while this can get tricky since it opens the floodgates for mentioning every close friend and great association and good-hearted soul who's ever shown me kindness, I hope they'll understand if I limit myself to those who had some direct impact on this book in particular, a few of whom I've never met and one or two whom I wouldn't know if they tapped me on the shoulder, all during a tumultuous moment of my life rocked by circumstantial insecurity. This work was born in a miraculous four-month period beginning one December morning in 2013 with a mysterious FedEx envelope that brought a lifesaving gift (if he's reading, he knows who he is) and ending the following April with a stupefying phone call from a well-known family foundation. These benefactors also included gracious hosts who gave me a place to work, living inspirations who taught me how to think and write, and generous champions who lent the book precious time and attention and went to the mat for it: Michael Ventura; Michael Silverblatt; Rick Moody; Jonathan Lethem; Joanna Scott; Kit Rachlis; Jeffrey Moskowitz; Richard Powers; Greil Marcus; Peter Guralnick; Susan Straight; Doug Aitken; Steve De

Jarnatt; Katherine Taylor; Nana Gregory; Alex Austin; Tom Carson; John Powers; Fred Cohn; Anthony Miller; Bruce Bauman; my Japanese translator Motoyuki Shibata and the staff of *Monkey Business*, in which pages a small part of the novel originally appeared in a different form; the Lannan Foundation, for whom my gratitude remains inarticulate; David Rosenthal, Katie Zaborsky, and the great people at Blue Rider, whose enthusiasm for the book from the first was unmarked by the bipolarity and mindfuckery that distinguishes some other publishers; and Melanie Jackson, my agent until the wheels come off, who took a chance on me half a lifetime ago when some couldn't see the point and who keeps doing it when others still can't. Finally, my family. Oh the woe of being related by law or blood to a writer, with his vacant stares at the dinner table, raging inner dramas behind the wheel of a car, emotional shutdowns following the unfortunate phone calls. We can pretend the family does it for literature but a better guess is they love me, and what in God's name, the egomaniacal author wonders, can *that* be about? My wife, Lori, my kids, Miles and Silanchi, and my mother, Joanna, didn't just make this book, they *are* this book, as almost anyone reading it will recognize whether they know me or not.

About the Author

STEVE ERICKSON is the author of nine other novels and two non-fiction books that have been published in ten languages. His work has appeared in numerous periodicals such as *Esquire*, *Rolling Stone*, *Smithsonian*, *American Prospect*, and *Los Angeles*, for which he writes regularly about film, music, and television, and for twelve years he was founding editor of the national literary journal *Black Clock*. Erickson is the recipient of a Guggenheim Fellowship, the American Academy of Arts and Letters award in literature, and the Lannan Lifetime Achievement Award. Currently he teaches at the University of California, Riverside.